# Stories and Poems
# for the Very Young

# STORIES AND POEMS
# FOR THE
# VERY YOUNG

Selected and with a Commentary by

BRYNA AND LOUIS UNTERMEYER

 Golden Press • New York

WESTERN PUBLISHING COMPANY, INC.
RACINE, WISCONSIN

## ACKNOWLEDGMENTS

The editors and publishers have made every effort to trace the ownership of all copyrighted material and to secure permission from the holders of the copyright. In the event of any question arising as to the use of any of the selections, the editors and publishers, while expressing regret for any inadvertent error, will be glad to make the necessary correction in future printings. Thanks are due to the following publishers, agents, owners of copyright, and authors for permission to reprint the material indicated.

The Cardavon Press, Inc. for "The Mouse's Wedding" from the Heritage Press edition of *The Complete Andersen,* translated by Jean Hersholt, copyright 1942 and 1949; reprinted by permission of The Cardavon Press, Inc., Avon, Connecticut 06001.

E. P. Dutton & Co., Inc. for text from the book *Peter Churchmouse* by Margot Austin. Copyright 1941 by E. P. Dutton & Co., Inc. Renewal © 1969 by Margot Austin. Published by E. P. Dutton & Co., Inc. and used with their permission.

Harcourt Brace Jovanovich, Inc. for "The Five Marvelous Pretzels" from *The Sandburg Range,* © 1957 by Carl Sandburg. Reprinted by permission of Harcourt Brace Jovanovich, Inc.

David Higham Associates, Ltd. for "Living in W'ales" by Richard Hughes, published by Chatto & Windus.

Longman Group Ltd. for "Little Half-Chick" from *The Green Fairy Book* edited by Andrew Lang.

Macmillan Publishing Co., Inc. for "Lazy Jack" and "The Story of the Three Bears," reprinted with permission of Macmillan Publishing Co., Inc. from *English Fairy Tales* by Flora Annie Steel. Copyright 1918 by Macmillan Publishing Co., Inc.; renewed 1946 by Mabel H. Webster. Reprinted also with the permission of Macmillan, London and Basingstoke.

Janet McNeill and Hamish Hamilton Ltd. for "The Small Brown Mouse" from *Dragons Come Home* by Janet McNeill. Reprinted by permission of the author and the publisher through the courtesy of A. P. Watt & Son.

Thomas Nelson Inc. for "How She Finished Her Red Muffler" and "How She Kept Her Geese Warm" from *The Little Old Woman Who Used Her Head* by Hope Newell, copyright 1935 by Hope Newell. Reprinted by permission of the publisher, Thomas Nelson Inc.

G. P. Putnam's Sons for "Henny-Penny," "Jack and the Beanstalk," "The Old Woman and Her Pig," "The Story of the Three Little Pigs," and "Teeny-Tiny." Reprinted by permission of G. P. Putnam's Sons from *English Folk and Fairy Tales* collected by Joseph Jacobs.

Charles Scribner's Sons for "Wynken, Blynken, and Nod" from *A Little Book of Western Verse* by Eugene Field.

Henry Z. Walck, Inc. and Oxford University Press (London) for "The Prince of the Seven Golden Cows" from *French Legends, Tales and Fairy Stories* by Barbara Leonie Picard; for "Simpleton Peter" from *English Fables and Fairy Stories* by James Reeves; for "The Water-Sprite and the Bear" from *German Hero-Sagas and Folk-Tales* by Barbara Leonie Picard, © 1958 Barbara Leonie Picard. Reprinted by permission of Henry Z. Walck, Inc. and Oxford University Press (London).

Frederick Warne & Co. Ltd. for *The Tale of Peter Rabbit,* story and illustrations by Beatrix Potter. Reprinted by permission of the publishers and The Beatrix Potter Estate.

The adaptations of various stories in this collection are © 1973 by Bryna and Louis Untermeyer.

# Contents

# Foreword

*Once upon a time—a long time ago—we, too, were very young.*
*Some of the stories we read were very old, but they were new to us.*
*In those stories many things happened that did not happen in real life.*
*But we believed they might happen—somehow, somewhere.*
*We wanted to believe that animals could talk, that three little pigs*
*could fool a big, bad wolf, that a billy-goat by the name of Gruff*
*could get the better of a wicked troll, that a small mouse*
*called Peter could write poetry. We fell in love with Henny-Penny*
*who was afraid the sky was going to fall and went to tell the king*
*about it with her friends Cocky-Locky, Ducky-Daddles, Goosey-Poosey,*
*Turkey-Lurkey...and how we hated Foxy-Woxy! We were sorry for*
*the naughty little Half-Chick who had to stand on one leg*
*on the top of the tall steeple.*
*And there were people who were just as strange as the*
*strange creatures they lived with. There was the little old woman*
*who used her head—but used it in the most foolish way.*
*There was Lazy Jack who did all sorts of things—and did them*
*all wrong. There was the cook who had trouble with a brownie.*
*And then there were the poems. Rhymes we repeated over*
*and over again—all the way from the jingles of Mother Goose*
*to "A Child's Garden of Verses" to "Wynken, Blynken, and Nod"*
*—until we knew all of them by heart.*
*We could not tire of stories and poems like these. We never will.*

BRYNA AND LOUIS UNTERMEYER

# Teeny-Tiny

### RETOLD BY JOSEPH JACOBS

Once upon a time there was a teeny-tiny woman who lived in a teeny-tiny house in a teeny-tiny village. Now, one day this teeny-tiny woman put on her teeny-tiny bonnet and went out of her teeny-tiny house to take a teeny-tiny walk. And when this teeny-tiny woman had gone a teeny-tiny way, she came to a teeny-tiny gate; so the teeny-tiny woman opened the teeny-tiny gate and went into a teeny-tiny churchyard. And when this teeny-tiny woman had got into the teeny-tiny churchyard, she saw a teeny-tiny bone on a teeny-tiny grave, and the teeny-tiny woman said to her teeny-tiny self, "This teeny-tiny bone will make me some teeny-tiny soup for my teeny-tiny supper." So the teeny-tiny woman put the teeny-tiny bone into her teeny-tiny pocket and went home to her teeny-tiny house.

8

Now when the teeny-tiny woman got home to her teeny-tiny house, she was a teeny-tiny bit tired; so she went up her teeny-tiny stairs to her teeny-tiny bed and put the teeny-tiny bone into a teeny-tiny cupboard. And when this teeny-tiny woman had been to sleep a teeny-tiny time, she was awakened by a teeny-tiny voice from the teeny-tiny cupboard, which said,

"Give me my bone!"

And this teeny-tiny woman was a teeny-tiny frightened; so she hid her teeny-tiny head under the teeny-tiny clothes and went to sleep again. And when she had been to sleep again a teeny-tiny time, the teeny-tiny voice again cried out from the teeny-tiny cupboard a teeny-tiny louder,

"Give me my bone!"

This made the teeny-tiny woman a teeny-tiny more frightened; so she hid her teeny-tiny head a teeny-tiny farther under the teeny-tiny clothes. And when the teeny-tiny woman had been to sleep again a teeny-tiny time, the teeny-tiny voice from the teeny-tiny cupboard said again a teeny-tiny louder,

"Give me my bone!"

And this teeny-tiny woman was a teeny-tiny bit more frightened, but she put her teeny-tiny head out of the teeny-tiny clothes and said in her loudest teeny-tiny voice, "TAKE IT!"

# Henny-Penny

### RETOLD BY JOSEPH JACOBS

One day Henny-Penny was walking under a tree in the woods when—whack!—something hit her upon the head. "Goodness gracious me!" said Henny-Penny; "the sky's a-going to fall; I must go and tell the king."

So she went along, and she went along, and she went along till she met Cocky-Locky. "Where are you going, Henny-Penny?" says Cocky-Locky. "Oh! I'm going to tell the king the sky's a-falling," says Henny-Penny. "May I come with you?" says Cocky-Locky. "Certainly," says Henny-Penny. So Henny-Penny and Cocky-Locky went to tell the king the sky was a-falling.

10

They went along, and they went along, and they went along till they met Ducky-Daddles. "Where are you going to, Henny-Penny and Cocky-Locky?" says Ducky-Daddles. "Oh! we're going to tell the king the sky's a-falling," said Henny-Penny and Cocky-Locky. "May I come with you?" says Ducky-Daddles. "Certainly," said Henny-Penny and Cocky-Locky. So Henny-Penny, Cocky-Locky, and Ducky-Daddles went to tell the king the sky was a-falling.

So they went along, and they went along, and they went along, till they met Goosey-Poosey. "Where are you going to, Henny-Penny, Cocky-Locky, and Ducky-Daddles?" said Goosey-Poosey. "Oh! we're going to tell the king the sky's a-falling," said Henny-Penny and Cocky-Locky and Ducky-Daddles. "May I come with you?" said Goosey-Poosey. "Certainly," said Henny-Penny, Cocky-Locky, and Ducky-Daddles. So Henny-Penny, Cocky-Locky, Ducky-Daddles, and Goosey-Poosey went to tell the king the sky was a-falling.

So they went along, and they went along, and they went along, till they met Turkey-Lurkey. "Where are you going, Henny-Penny, Cocky-Locky, Ducky-Daddles, and Goosey-Poosey?" says Turkey-Lurkey. "Oh! we're going to tell the king the sky's a-falling," said Henny-Penny, Cocky-Locky, Ducky-Daddles, and Goosey-Poosey. "May I come with you, Henny-Penny, Cocky-Locky, Ducky-Daddles, and Goosey-Poosey?" said Turkey-Lurkey. "Oh, certainly, Turkey-Lurkey," said Henny-Penny, Cocky-Locky, Ducky-Daddles, and Goosey-Poosey. So Henny-Penny, Cocky-Locky, Ducky-Daddles, Goosey-Poosey, and Turkey-Lurkey all went to tell the king the sky was a-falling.

So they went along, and they went along, and they went along, till they met Foxy-Woxy; and Foxy-Woxy said to Henny-Penny, Cocky-Locky, Ducky-Daddles, Goosey-Poosey, and Turkey-Lurkey: "Where are you going, Henny-Penny, Cocky-Locky, Ducky-Daddles, Goosey-Poosey, and Turkey-Lurkey?" And Henny-Penny, Cocky-Locky, Ducky-Daddles, Goosey-Poosey, and Turkey-Lurkey said to Foxy-Woxy: "We're going to tell the king the sky's a-falling." "Oh! but this is not the way to the king, Henny-Penny, Cocky-Locky, Ducky-Daddles, Goosey-Poosey,

and Turkey-Lurkey," says Foxy-Woxy; "I know the proper way; shall I show it you?" "Oh, certainly, Foxy-Woxy," said Henny-Penny, Cocky-Locky, Ducky-Daddles, Goosey-Poosey, and Turkey-Lurkey. So Henny-Penny, Cocky-Locky, Ducky-Daddles, Goosey-Poosey, Turkey-Lurkey, and Foxy-Woxy all went to tell the king the sky was a-falling. So they went along, and they went along, and they went along, till they came to a narrow and dark hole. Now this was the door of Foxy-Woxy's cave. But Foxy-Woxy said to Henny-Penny, Cocky-Locky, Ducky-Daddles, Goosey-Poosey, and Turkey-Lurkey: "This is the short way to the king's palace; you'll soon get there if you follow me. I will go first and you come after, Henny-Penny, Cocky-Locky, Ducky-Daddles, Goosey-Poosey, and Turkey-Lurkey." "Why of course, certainly, without doubt, why not?" said Henny-Penny, Cocky-Locky, Ducky-Daddles, Goosey-Poosey, and Turkey-Lurkey.

So Foxy-Woxy went into his cave, and he didn't go very far, but turned round to wait for Henny-Penny, Cocky-Locky, Ducky-Daddles, Goosey-Poosey, and Turkey-Lurkey. So at last at first Turkey-Lurkey went through the dark hole into the cave. He hadn't got far when "Hrumph," Foxy-Woxy snapped off Turkey-Lurkey's head and threw his body over his left shoulder. Then Goosey-Poosey went in, and "Hrumph," off went her head and Goosey-Poosey was thrown beside Turkey-Lurkey. Then Ducky-Daddles waddled down, and "Hrumph," snapped Foxy-Woxy, and Ducky-Daddles' head was off and Ducky-Daddles was thrown alongside Turkey-Lurkey and Goosey-Poosey. Then, Cocky-Locky strutted down into the cave, and he hadn't gone far when "Snap, Hrumph!" went Foxy-Woxy and Cocky-Locky was thrown alongside of Turkey-Lurkey, Goosey-Poosey, and Ducky-Daddles.

But Foxy-Woxy had made two bites at Cocky-Locky; and when the first snap only hurt Cocky-Locky, but didn't kill him, he called out to Henny-Penny. But she turned tail and off she ran home; so she never told the king the sky was a-falling.

14

# The Story
# of the Three Little Pigs

### RETOLD BY JOSEPH JACOBS

Once upon a time when pigs spoke rhyme
And monkeys chewed tobacco,
And hens took snuff to make them tough,
And ducks went quack, quack, quack, O!
There was an old sow with three little pigs, and as she had not enough to keep them, she sent them out to seek their fortune. The first that went off met a man with a bundle of straw, and said to him,

"Please, man, give me that straw to build me a house."

Which the man did, and the little pig built a house with it. Presently along came a wolf, and knocked at the door, and said,

"Little pig, little pig, let me come in."

To which the pig answered,

"No, no, by the hair of my chiny chin chin."

The wolf then answered to that,

"Then I'll huff, and I'll puff, and I'll blow your house in."

So he huffed, and he puffed, and he blew his house in, and ate up the little pig.

The second little pig met a man with a bundle of furze and said,

"Please, man, give me that furze to build a house."

Which the man did, and the pig built his house. Then along came the wolf, and said,

"Little pig, little pig, let me come in."

"No, no, by the hair of my chiny chin chin."

"Then I'll puff, and I'll huff, and I'll blow your house in."

So he huffed, and he puffed, and he puffed, and he huffed, and at last he blew the house down, and he ate up the little pig.

The third little pig met a man with a load of bricks, and said, "Please, man, give me those bricks to build a house with."

So the man gave him the bricks, and he built his house with them. So the wolf came, as he did to the other little pigs, and said,

"Little pig, little pig, let me come in."

"No, no, by the hair on my chiny chin chin."

"Then I'll huff, and I'll puff, and I'll blow your house in."

Well, he huffed, and he puffed, and he huffed and he puffed, and he

puffed and huffed; but he could *not* get the house down. When he found
that he could not, with all his huffing and puffing, blow the house down,
he said,

"Little pig, I know where there is a nice field of turnips."

"Where?" said the little pig.

"Oh, in Mr. Smith's home-field, and if you will be ready tomorrow
morning I will call for you, and we will go together, and get some for
dinner."

"Very well," said the little pig, "I will be ready. What time do you
mean to go?"

"Oh, at six o'clock."

Well, the little pig got up at five and got the turnips before the wolf came (which he did about six), who said,

"Little pig, are you ready?"

The little pig said, "Ready! I have been and come back again and got a nice potful for dinner."

The wolf felt very angry at this, but thought that he would be up to the little pig somehow or other, so he said,

"Little pig, I know where there is a nice apple-tree."

"Where?" said the pig.

"Down at Merry-Garden," replied the wolf, "and if you will not deceive me, I will come for you at five o'clock tomorrow and get some apples."

Well, the little pig bustled up the next morning at four o'clock, and went off for the apples, hoping to get back before the wolf came; but he had farther to go and had to climb the tree, so that just as he was coming down from it, he saw the wolf coming which, as you may suppose, frightened him very much. When the wolf came up he said:

"Little pig, what! are you here before me? Are they nice apples?"

"Yes, very," said the little pig. "I will throw you down one."

And he threw it so far, that, while the wolf was gone to pick it up, the little pig jumped down and ran home. The next day the wolf came again and said to the little pig,

"Little pig, there is a fair at Shanklin this afternoon; will you go?"

"Oh, yes," said the pig, "I will go; what time shall you be ready?"

"At three," said the wolf. So the little pig went off before the time as usual and got to the fair and bought a butter-churn, which he was going home with, when he saw the wolf coming. Then he could not tell what to do. So he got into the churn to hide, and by so doing turned it round, and it rolled down the hill with the pig in it, which frightened the wolf so much, that he ran home without going to the fair. He went to the little pig's house and told him how frightened he had been by a great

19

round thing which came down the hill past him. Then the little pig said,

"Hah, I frightened you then. I had been to the fair and bought a butter-churn; and when I saw you, I got into it, and rolled down the hill."

Then the wolf was very angry indeed and declared he *would* eat up the little pig, and that he would get down the chimney after him. When the little pig saw what he was about, he hung on the pot full of water and made up a blazing fire and, just as the wolf was coming down, took off the cover and in fell the wolf; so the little pig put on the cover again in an instant, boiled him up, and ate him for supper and lived happy ever afterwards.

# The Old Woman and Her Pig

### RETOLD BY JOSEPH JACOBS

An old woman was sweeping her house, and she found a little crooked sixpence. "What," said she, "shall I do with this little sixpence? I will go to market, and buy a little pig."

As she was coming home, she came to a stile: but the piggy wouldn't go over the stile.

She went a little further, and she met a dog. So she said to him: "Dog! dog! bite pig; piggy won't go over the stile; and I shan't get home tonight." But the dog wouldn't.

She went a little further, and she met a stick. So she said: "Stick! stick! beat dog! dog won't bite pig; piggy won't get over the stile; and I shan't get home tonight." But the stick wouldn't.

She went a little further, and she met a fire. So she said: "Fire! fire! burn stick; stick won't beat dog; dog won't bite pig; piggy won't get over the stile; and I shan't get home tonight." But the fire wouldn't.

She went a little further, and she met some water. So she said: "Water! water! quench fire; fire won't burn stick; stick won't beat dog; dog won't bite pig; piggy won't get over the stile; and I shan't get home tonight." But the water wouldn't.

She went a little further, and she met an ox. So she said: "Ox! ox! drink water; water won't quench fire; fire won't burn stick; stick won't beat dog; dog won't bite pig; piggy won't get over the stile; and I shan't get home tonight." But the ox wouldn't.

She went a little further, and she met a butcher. So she said: "Butcher! butcher! kill ox; ox won't drink water; water won't quench fire; fire won't burn stick; stick won't beat dog; dog won't bite pig; piggy won't get over the stile; and I shan't get home tonight." But the butcher wouldn't.

She went a little further, and she met a rope. So she

said: "Rope! rope! hang butcher; butcher won't kill ox; ox won't drink water; water won't quench fire; fire won't burn stick; stick won't beat dog; dog won't bite pig; piggy won't get over the stile; and I shan't get home tonight." But the rope wouldn't.

She went a little further, and she met a rat. So she said: "Rat! rat! gnaw rope; rope won't hang butcher; butcher won't kill ox; ox won't drink water; water won't quench fire; fire won't burn stick; stick won't beat dog; dog won't bite pig; piggy won't get over the stile; and I shan't get home tonight." But the rat wouldn't.

She went a little further, and she met a cat. So she said: "Cat! cat! kill rat; rat won't gnaw rope; rope won't hang butcher; butcher won't kill ox; ox won't drink water; water won't quench fire; fire won't burn stick; stick won't beat dog; dog won't bite pig; piggy won't get over the stile; and I shan't get home tonight." But the cat said to her, "If you

will go to yonder cow, and fetch me a saucer of milk, I will kill the rat." So away went the old woman to the cow.

But the cow said to her: "If you will go to yonder hay-stack and fetch me a handful of hay, I'll give you the milk." So away went the old woman to the hay-stack; and she brought the hay to the cow.

As soon as the cow had eaten the hay, she gave the old woman the milk; and away she went with it in a saucer to the cat.

As soon as the cat had lapped up the milk, the cat began to kill the rat; the rat began to gnaw the rope; the rope began to hang the butcher; the butcher began to kill the ox; the ox began to drink the water; the water began to quench the fire; the fire began to burn the stick; the stick began to beat the dog; the dog began to bite the pig; the little pig in a fright jumped over the stile; and so the old woman got home that night.

# Little Red Riding Hood

BY CHARLES PERRAULT • RETOLD BY LOUIS UNTERMEYER

Once upon a time a little girl lived in a small village ever so far away. She was very pretty and sweet-tempered; her mother loved her dearly, and her grandmother loved her even more. This good old woman made her granddaughter a little red hood, which fitted her so well that everybody called her "Little Red Riding Hood."

One day her mother made some cheesecakes. Calling her little girl she said, "I have heard that your grandmother is not well; I wish you would go and see how she is today, and carry her a cheesecake and this little pot of butter. And, mind, do not stop to talk with anyone on the way."

So Little Red Riding Riding Hood took the cheesecake and the pot of butter, and set out to visit her grandmother, who lived in another village. Going through the woods she met a wolf who walked along beside her, and wanted to eat her up. But he did not dare to, being afraid of some

wood-cutters who were in the forest. He asked her where she was going. The poor child, who did not know that it was dangerous to stop and listen to a wolf, replied:

"I am going to see my grandmother, and bring her this cheesecake and little pot of butter from my mother."

"Does she live very far away?" inquired the wolf.

"Oh, yes," said Little Red Riding Hood, "it is beyond the mill which you see away down there—the first house in the village."

"Oh, well," said the wolf, "I think I'll go and see her too. I will go by this road, and you go by that, and we shall see who gets there first."

28

The wolf ran at top speed by the shortest road, and the little girl went by the longest road, amusing herself by gathering nuts, chasing butter-flies, and making bouquets of the wild flowers which she picked in the woods.

The wolf was not long in finding his way to the cottage, and knocked at the door.

"Who's there?" asked the grandmother.

"It is your grandchild, Little Red Riding Hood," said the wolf, imitating her voice, "and I have brought a cheesecake and a little pot of butter for you, which mother has sent."

The good grandmother, who had gone to bed because she was not very well, called out:

"Pull the bobbin, and the latch will fly up."

The wolf pulled the string and the door flew open. He leaped upon the good woman and ate her up. Then he lay down in the grandmother's bed and waited for Little Red Riding Hood. Soon she came and knocked at the door.

"Who's there?" said he.

Little Red Riding Hood, hearing the rough voice of the wolf, was afraid at first. But she supposed her grandmother had a bad cold and she replied:

"It is your grandchild, Little Red Riding Hood, and I have brought you a cheesecake and a little pot of butter, which mother has sent to you."

The wolf called out, softening his voice a little, "Pull the bobbin, and the latch will fly up."

Little Red Riding Hood pulled the bobbin, and the door flew open. The wolf, seeing her come in, hid himself under the bedclothes, and said to her, "Put the cake and the pot of butter upon the table, and come and lie down with me, for you must be very tired."

So Little Red Riding Hood undressed herself, and got into bed. But she was frightened to see how strange her grandmother looked. She cried out:

"Grandmother, what great arms you have!"

And the wolf replied, "The better to hug you with, my child."

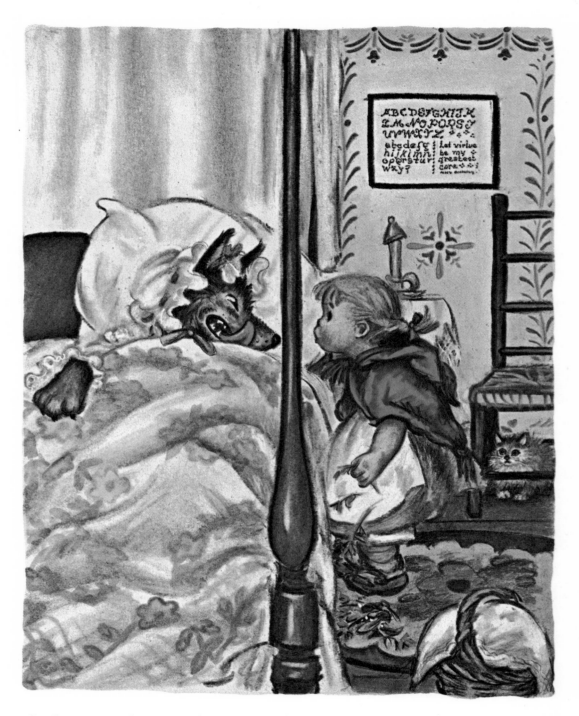

"What great legs you have, grandmother!"
"The better to run with, my child."
"What great ears you have, grandmother!"

"The better to hear you with, my child."

"What great eyes you have, grandmother!"

"The better to see you with, my child."

"What great teeth you have, grandmother!"

"The better to eat you with!"

And with these words, the wicked wolf sprang upon Little Red Riding Hood, and swallowed her.

A hunter passing the house had heard Little Red Riding Hood scream. Opening the door he saw the wolf with the grandmother's nightcap on, and raised his gun to shoot. Then he remembered the scream. Drawing his knife before the wolf could spring at him, he cut open the wicked creature. What was his surprise when Little Red Riding Hood jumped out, crying, "How frightened I was! It was so dark inside!"

The grandmother was pulled out next, a little out of breath but still alive.

The huntsman skinned the wolf and gave the skin to the grandmother for a winter coat. Then they all sat down to eat the cake and the little pot of butter. And Little Red Riding Hood said, "I will never again forget what my mother told me. Never again will I talk to strangers."

*This is the first story in a book*
*called "The Adventures of a Brownie."*
*Brownies are rare—very few families have one.*
*But any family is lucky that can claim one*
*as mischievous, yet as tidy,*
*and altogether as nice as this particular Brownie.*

# The Brownie and the Cook

## BY DINAH MULOCK CRAIK

There was once a little Brownie who lived—where do you think he lived?—in a coal cellar.

Now a coal cellar may seem a most curious place to choose to live in; but then a Brownie is a curious creature—a fairy, yet not one of that sort of fairies who fly about on gossamer wings, and dance in the moonlight, and so on. He never dances; and as to wings, what use would they be to him in a coal cellar? He is a sober, stay-at-home household elf—nothing much to look at, even if you did see him, which you are not likely to do—only a little old man, about a foot high, all dressed in brown, with a brown face and hands, and brown peaked cap, just the color of a brown mouse. And like a mouse he hides in corners—especially kitchen corners, and only comes out after dark when nobody is about, and so sometimes people call him Mr. Nobody.

I said you were not likely to see him; I never did, certainly, and never knew anybody that did, but still, if you were to go into Devonshire, you would hear many funny stories about Brownies in general. So I may as well tell you the adventures of one particular Brownie, who belonged to a family there; which family he had followed from house to house, most faithfully, for years and years. A good many people had heard him—or supposed they had—when there were extraordinary noises about the house; noises which must have come from a mouse or a rat—or a Brownie. But nobody had ever seen him, except the children, the three little boys and three little girls—who declared he often came to play with them when they were alone, and was the nicest companion in the world, though he was such an old man—hundreds of years old! He was full of fun and mischief, and up to all sorts of tricks; but he never did anybody any harm—unless they deserved it.

Brownie was supposed to live under one particular coal, in the darkest corner of the cellar, which was never allowed to be disturbed. Why he had chosen it nobody knew, and how he lived there, nobody knew either; nor what he lived upon. Except that, ever since the family could remember, there had always been a bowl of milk put behind the coal cellar door for the Brownie's supper. Perhaps he drank it—perhaps he didn't: anyhow, the bowl was always found empty next morning.

The old Cook, who had lived all her life in the family, had never once forgotten to give Brownie his supper; but at last she died, and a young Cook came in her stead, who was very apt to forget everything. She was also both careless and lazy, and disliked taking the trouble to put a bowl of milk in the same place every night for Mr. Nobody. "I don't believe in Brownies," she said; "I have never seen one, and seeing's believing." So she laughed at the other servants, who looked very grave, and put the bowl of milk in its place as often as they could, without saying much about it.

But once, when Brownie woke up, at his usual hour for rising—ten o'clock at night—and looked round in search of his supper—which was in fact his breakfast—he found nothing there. At first he could not imagine such neglect, and went smelling and smelling about for his bowl of milk —it was not always placed in the same corner now—but in vain.

"This will never do," said he; and being extremely hungry, began running about the coal cellar to see what he could find. His eyes were as useful in the dark as in the light—like a pussycat's; but there was nothing to be seen— not even a potato paring, or a dry crust, or a well-gnawed bone, such as Tiny the terrier sometimes brought into the coal cellar and left on the floor. Nothing, in short, but heaps of coals and coal dust, which even a Brownie cannot eat, you know.

"Can't stand this; quite impossible!" said the Brownie, tightening his belt to make his poor little inside feel less empty. He had been asleep so long—about a week, I believe, as was his habit when there was nothing to do—that he seemed ready to eat his own head, or his boots, or anything. "What's to be done? Since nobody brings my supper I must go and fetch it."

He spoke quickly, for he always thought quickly, and made up his mind in a minute. To be sure it was a very little mind, like his little body, but he did the best he could with it, and was not a bad sort of old fellow after all. In the house he had never done any harm—and often some good, for he frightened away all the rats, mice, and black beetles. Not the crickets—he liked them, as the old Cook had done; she said they were such cheerful creatures, and always brought luck to the house. But the young Cook could not bear them, and used to pour boiling water down their holes, and set basins of beer with little wooden bridges up to the rim, that they might walk up, tumble in, and be drowned.

So there was not even a cricket singing in the silent house when Brownie put his head out of his coal cellar door, which, to his surprise, he found open. Old Cook used to lock it every night; but the young Cook had left that key, and kitchen and pantry keys too, all dangling in the lock, so that any thief might have got in, and wandered all over the house without being found out.

"Hurrah, here's luck!" cried Brownie, tossing his cap up in the air and bounding right through the scullery into the kitchen. It was quite empty, but there was a good fire burning itself out, just for its own amusement, and the remains of a capital supper were spread on the table— enough for a half-dozen people.

Would you like to know what there was? Devonshire cream, of course; and part of a large dish of junket, which is something like curds and whey. Lots of bread and butter and cheese, and half an apple pudding. Also a great jug of cider and another of milk, and several half-full glasses, and no end of dirty plates, knives, and forks. All were scattered about the table in the most untidy fashion, just as the servants had risen from their supper, without thinking to put anything away.

Brownie screwed up his little old face and turned up his button of a nose, and gave a long whistle. You might not believe it, seeing he lived in a coal cellar, but really he liked tidiness, and always played his pranks upon disorderly or slovenly folk.

"Whew!" said he. "Here's a chance! What a supper I'll get now!"

And he jumped on to a chair and thence to the table, but so quietly that the large black cat with four white paws (called Muff, because she was so fat and soft and her fur so long), who sat dozing in front of the fire, just opened one eye and went to sleep again. She had tried to get her nose into the milk jug, but it was too small; and the junket dish was too deep for her to reach, except with one paw. She didn't care much for bread and cheese and apple pudding, and was very well fed besides; so after wandering round the table she had jumped down from it, and settled herself to sleep on the hearth.

But Brownie had no notion of going to sleep. He wanted his supper, and oh! what a supper he did eat; first one thing and then another, and then trying everything all over again. And oh! what a lot he drank!—first milk and then cider, and then mixed the two together in a way that would have disagreed with anybody except a Brownie. As it was, he was obliged to slacken his belt several times, and at last took it off altogether. But he must have had a most extraordinary capacity for eating and drinking since, after he had cleared off all the food, he was just as lively as ever, and began jumping about on the table as if he had had no supper at all.

His jumping was a little unfortunate, for there happened

to be a clean white tablecloth; as this was only Monday, it had had no time to get dirty—untidy as the Cook was. And you know Brownie lived in a coal cellar, and his feet were black with running about in coal dust. So wherever he trod, he left the impression behind; until at last the whole tablecloth was covered with black marks.

Not that he minded this; in fact, he took great pains to make the cloth as dirty as possible. And then laughing loudly "Ho, ho, ho!" leaped on to the hearth, and began teasing the cat; squeaking like a mouse, or chirping like a cricket, or buzzing like a fly; and altogether disturbing poor Pussy's mind so much that she went and hid herself in the farthest corner, and left him the hearth all to himself, where he lay at ease till daybreak.

Then, hearing a slight noise overhead, which might be the servants getting up, he jumped on to the table again—gobbled up the few remaining crumbs for his breakfast, and scampered off to his coal cellar, where he hid himself under his big coal, and fell asleep for the day.

Well, the Cook came downstairs rather earlier than usual, for she remembered she had to clear off the remains of supper; but lo and behold, there was nothing left to clear! Every bit of food was eaten up—the cheese looked as if a dozen mice had been nibbling at it, and nibbled it down to the very rind; the milk and cider were all gone—and mice don't care for milk and cider, you know; as for the apple pudding, it had vanished altogether; and the dish was licked as clean as if Boxer the yard dog had been at it in his hungriest mood.

"And my white tablecloth—oh, my clean white tablecloth! What can have been done to it?" cried she in amazement. For it was all over little black footmarks, just the size of a baby's foot—only babies don't wear shoes with nails in them, and don't run about and climb on kitchen tables after all the family have gone to bed.

Cook was a little frightened; but her fright changed to anger when she saw the large black cat stretched comfortably on the hearth. Poor Muff had crept there for a little snooze after Brownie went away.

"You nasty cat! I see it all now; it's you that have eaten up all the supper; it's you that have been on my clean tablecloth with your dirty paws."

They were white paws, and as clean as possible; but Cook never thought of that, any more than she did of the fact that cats don't usually drink cider or eat apple pudding.

"I'll teach you to come stealing food in this way; take that—that—and that!"

Cook got hold of a broom and beat poor Pussy till the creature ran mewing away. She couldn't speak, you know—unfortunate cat! and tell people that it was Brownie who had done it all.

Next night Cook thought she would make all safe and sure; so, instead of letting the cat sleep by the fire, she shut her up in the chill coal cellar, locked the door, put the key in her pocket, and went off to bed, leaving the supper as before.

40

When Brownie woke up and looked out of his hole, there was, as usual, no supper for him, and the cellar was closed shut. He peered about, to try to find some cranny under the door to creep out at, but there was none. And he felt so hungry that he could almost have eaten the cat, who kept walking to and fro in a melancholy manner—only she was alive, and he couldn't well eat her alive; besides, he knew she was old, and had an idea she might be tough. So he merely said politely, "How do you do, Mrs. Pussy?" to which she answered nothing—of course.

Something must be done, and luckily Brownies can do things that nobody else can do. So he thought he would change himself into a mouse, and gnaw a hole through the door. But then he suddenly remembered the cat, who, though he had decided not to eat her, might take this opportunity of eating him. So he thought it advisable to wait till she was fast asleep, which did not happen for a good while. At length, quite tired with walking about, Pussy turned round on her tail six times, curled down in a corner, and fell fast asleep.

Immediately Brownie changed himself into the smallest mouse possible; and, taking care not to make the least noise, gnawed a hole in the door, and squeezed himself through—immediately turning into his proper shape again, for fear of accidents.

The kitchen fire was at its last glimmer; but there was a better supper than even last night, for the Cook had had friends with her, a brother and two cousins, and they had been exceedingly merry. The food they had left behind was enough for three Brownies at least, but this one managed to eat it all up. Only once, in trying to cut a great slice of beef, he let the carving knife and fork fall with such a clatter that Tiny the terrier, who was tied up at the foot of the stairs, began to bark furiously. However, he brought her her puppy, which had been left in a basket in a corner of the kitchen, and so succeeded in quieting the dog.

After that he enjoyed himself amazingly, and made more marks than ever on the white tablecloth, for he began jumping about like a pea on a trencher, in order to make his particularly large supper agree with him.

Then, in the absence of the cat, he teased the puppy for an hour or two, till, hearing the clock strike five, he thought it as well to turn into a mouse again, and creep back cautiously into his cellar. He was only just in time, for Muff opened one eye, and was just going to pounce upon him, when he changed himself back into a Brownie. She was so startled that she bounded away, her tail growing into twice its natural size and her eyes gleaming like round green globes. But Brownie only said, "Ha, ha, ho!" and walked deliberately into his hole.

When Cook came downstairs and saw that the same thing had happened again—that the supper was all eaten, and the tablecloth blacker than ever with the extraordinary footmarks, she was greatly puzzled. Who could have done it all? Not the cat, who came mewing out of the coal cellar the minute she unlocked the door. Possibly a rat—but then would a rat have come within reach of Tiny?

"It must have been Tiny herself, or her puppy," which just came rolling out of its basket over Cook's feet. "You little wretch! you and your mother are the greatest nuisance imaginable. I'll punish you!"

And quite forgetting that Tiny had been safely tied up all night, and that her poor little puppy was so fat and helpless it could scarcely stand on its legs—and so was unlikely to jump on chairs and tables—she gave them both such a thrashing that they ran howling together out of the kitchen door, where the kind little kitchen maid took them up in her arms.

"You ought to have beaten the Brownie, if you could catch him," said she indignantly. "He'll do it again and again, you'll see, for he can't bear an untidy kitchen. You'd better do as poor old Cook did, and clear the supper things away, and put the odds and ends safe in the larder. Also," she added mysteriously, "if I were you, I'd put a bowl of milk behind the coal cellar door."

"Nonsense!" answered the young Cook, and flounced away. But afterwards she thought better of it, and did as she was advised, grumbling all the time, but doing it.

Next morning, the milk was gone! Perhaps Brownie had drunk it up; anyhow, nobody could say that he hadn't. As for the supper, Cook having safely laid it on the shelves of the larder, nobody touched it. And the tablecloth, which was wrapped up tidily and put in the dresser drawer, came out as clean as ever, with not a single black footmark upon it. No mischief being done, the cat and the dog both escaped beating, and Brownie played no more tricks with anybody—till the next time.

# The Cock, the Mouse, and the Little Red Hen

### BY FÉLICITÉ LEFÈVRE

Once upon a time there was a hill, and on the hill there was a pretty little house.

It had one little green door, and four little windows with green shutters, and in it there lived A COCK, and A MOUSE, and A LITTLE RED HEN. On another hill close by, there was another little house. It was very ugly. It had a door that wouldn't shut, and two broken windows, and all the paint was off the shutters. And in this house there lived A BOLD BAD FOX and FOUR BAD LITTLE FOXES.

One morning these four bad little foxes came to the big bad Fox and said:

"Oh, Father, we're so hungry!"

"We had nothing to eat yesterday," said one.

"And scarcely anything the day before," said another.

The big bad Fox shook his head, for he was thinking. At last he said in a big gruff voice:

"On the hill over there I see a house. And in that house there lives a Cock."

"And a Mouse!" screamed two of the little foxes.

"And a little Red Hen," screamed the other two.

"And they are nice and fat," went on the big bad Fox. "This very day I'll take my sack and I will go up that hill and in at that door, and into my sack I will put the Cock, and the Mouse, and the little Red Hen."

So the four little foxes jumped for joy, and the big bad Fox went to get his sack ready to start upon his journey.

But what was happening to the Cock, and the Mouse, and the little Red Hen, all this time?

Well, sad to say, the Cock and the Mouse had both got out of bed on the wrong side that morning. The Cock said the day was too hot, and the Mouse grumbled because it was too cold.

They came grumbling down to the kitchen, where the good little Red Hen, looking as bright as a sunbeam, was bustling about.

"Who'll get some sticks to light the fire with?" she asked.

"I shan't," said the Cock.

"I shan't," said the Mouse.

"Then I'll do it myself," said the little Red Hen.

So off she ran to get the sticks. "And now, who'll fill the kettle from the spring?" she asked.

"I shan't," said the Cock.

"I shan't," said the Mouse.

"Then I'll do it myself," said the little Red Hen.

And off she ran to fill the kettle.

"And who'll get the breakfast ready?" she asked, as she put the kettle on to boil.

"I shan't," said the Cock.

"I shan't," said the Mouse.

"Then I'll do it myself," said the little Red Hen.

All breakfast time the Cock and the Mouse quarrelled and grumbled. The Cock upset the milk jug, and the Mouse scattered crumbs upon the floor.

"Who'll clear away the breakfast?" asked the poor little Red Hen, hoping they would soon leave off being cross.

"I shan't," said the Cock.

"I shan't," said the Mouse.

"Then I'll do it myself," said the little Red Hen.

So she cleared everything away, swept up the crumbs and brushed up the fireplace.

"And now, who'll help me to make the beds?"

"I shan't," said the Cock.

"I shan't," said the Mouse.

"Then I'll do it myself," said the little Red Hen.

And she tripped away upstairs.

But the lazy Cock and Mouse each sat down in a comfortable arm-chair by the fire, and soon fell fast asleep.

Now the bad Fox had crept up the hill and into the garden, and if the Cock and Mouse hadn't been asleep, they would have seen his sharp eyes peeping in at the window.

"Rat tat tat! Rat tat tat!" the Fox knocked at the door.

"Who can that be?" said the Mouse, half opening his eyes.

"Go and look for yourself, if you want to know," said the rude Cock.

"It's the postman perhaps," thought the Mouse to himself, "and he may have a letter for me." So without waiting to see who it was, he lifted the latch and opened the door.

As soon as he opened it, in jumped the big Fox.

"Oh! oh! oh!" squeaked the Mouse, as he tried to run up the chimney.

"Doodle doodle do!" screamed the Cock, as he jumped on the back of the biggest arm-chair.

But the Fox only laughed, and without more ado he took the little Mouse by the tail, and popped him into the sack, and seized the Cock by the neck and popped him in too.

Then the poor little Red Hen came running downstairs to see what all the noise was about, and the Fox caught her and put her into the sack with the others.

Then he took a long piece of string out of his pocket, wound it round, and round, and round the mouth of the sack, and tied it very tight indeed. After that he threw the sack over his back, and off he set down the hill, chuckling to himself.

"Oh, I wish I hadn't been so cross," said the Cock, as they went bumping about.

"Oh! I wish I hadn't been so lazy," said the Mouse, wiping his eyes with the tip of his tail.

"It's never too late to mend," said the little Red Hen. "And don't be too sad. See, here I have my little workbag, and in it there is a pair of scissors, and a little thimble, and a needle and thread. Very soon you will see what I am going to do."

Now the sun was very hot, and soon Mr. Fox began to

feel his sack was heavy, and at last he thought he would lie down under a tree and go to sleep for a little while. So he threw the sack down with a big bump, and very soon fell fast asleep.

Snore, snore, snore, went the Fox.

As soon as the little Red Hen heard this, she took out her scissors, and began to snip a hole in the sack just large enough for the Mouse to creep through.

"Quick," she whispered to the Mouse, "run as fast as you can and bring back a stone just as large as yourself."

Out scampered the Mouse, and soon came back, dragging the stone after him.

"Push it in here," said the little Red Hen, and he pushed it in, in a twinkling.

Then the little Red Hen snipped away at the hole, till it was large enough for the Cock to get through.

"Quick," she said, "run and get a stone as big as yourself."

Out flew the Cock, and soon came back quite out of breath, with a big stone, which he pushed into the sack too.

Then the little Red Hen popped out, got a stone as big as herself, and pushed it in. Next she put on her thimble, took out her needle and thread, and sewed up the hole as quickly as ever she could.

When it was done, the Cock, and the Mouse and the little Red Hen ran home very fast, shut the door after them, drew the bolts, shut the shutters, and drew down the blinds and felt quite safe.

The bad Fox lay fast asleep under the tree for some time, but at last he awoke.

"Dear, dear," he said, rubbing his eyes and then looking at the long shadows on the grass, "how late it is getting. I must hurry home."

So the bad Fox went grumbling and groaning down the hill, till he came to the stream. Splash! In went one foot. Splash! In went the other, but the stones in the sack were so heavy that at the very next step, down tumbled Mr. Fox into a deep pool. And then the fishes carried him off to their fairy caves and kept him a prisoner there, so he was never seen again. And the four greedy little foxes had to go to bed without any supper.

But the Cock and the Mouse never grumbled again. They lit the fire, filled the kettle, laid the breakfast, and did all the work, while the good little Red Hen had a holiday, and sat resting in the big arm-chair.

No foxes ever troubled them again, and for all I know they are still living happily in the little house with the green door and green shutters, which stands on the hill.

# Jack and the Beanstalk

### RETOLD BY JOSEPH JACOBS

There was once upon a time a poor widow who had a son named Jack and a cow named Milky-White. And all they had to live on was the milk the cow gave every morning, which they carried to the market and sold. But one morning Milky-White gave no milk, and they didn't know what to do.

"What shall we do, what shall we do?" said the widow.

"Cheer up, mother, I'll go and get work somewhere," said Jack.

"We've tried that before, and nobody would take you," said his.

50

mother; "we must sell Milky-White and with the money start shop or something."

"All right, mother," says Jack; "it's market-day today, and I'll soon sell Milky-White, and then we'll see what we can do."

So he took the cow's halter in his hand, and off he started. He hadn't gone far when he met a funny-looking old man, who said to him: "Good morning, Jack."

"Good morning to you," said Jack, and wondered how he knew his name.

"Well, Jack, and where are you off to?" said the man.

"I'm going to market to sell our cow here."

"Oh, you look the proper sort of chap to sell cows," said the man; "I wonder if you know how many beans make five."

"Two in each hand and one in your mouth," says Jack, as sharp as a needle.

"Right you are," says the man, "and here they are, the very beans themselves," he went on, pulling out of his pocket a number of strange-looking beans. "As you are so sharp," says he, "I don't mind doing a swap with you—your cow for these beans."

"Go along," says Jack; "wouldn't you like it?"

"Ah! you don't know what these beans are," said the man, "if you plant them overnight, by morning they grow right up to the sky."

"Really?" said Jack; "you don't say so."

"Yes, that is so, and if it doesn't turn out to be true you can have your cow back."

"Right," says Jack, and hands him over Milky-White's halter.

Back goes Jack home, and as he hadn't gone very far, it wasn't dusk by the time he got to his door.

"Back already, Jack?" said his mother; "I see you haven't got Milky-White, so you've sold her. How much did you get for her?"

"You'll never guess, mother," says Jack.

"No, you don't say so. Good boy! Five pounds, ten, fifteen, no, it can't be twenty."

"I told you you couldn't guess. What do you say to these beans; they're magical, plant them over-night and—"

"What!" says Jack's mother, "have you been such a fool, such a dolt, such an idiot, as to give away my Milky-White, the best milker in the parish, and prime beef to boot, for a set of paltry beans? Take that! Take that! Take that! And as for your precious beans here they go out of the window. And now off with you to bed. Not a sup shall you drink, and not a bit shall you swallow this very night."

So Jack went upstairs to his little room in the attic, and sad and sorry he was, to be sure, as much for his mother's sake, as for the loss of his supper. At last he dropped off to sleep.

When he woke up, the room looked so funny. The sun was shining into part of it, and yet all the rest was quite dark and shady. So Jack jumped up and dressed himself and went to the window. And what do you think he saw? Why, the beans his mother had thrown out of the window into the garden had sprung up into a big beanstalk, which went up and up and up till it reached the sky. So the man spoke truth after all.

The beanstalk grew up quite close past Jack's window; so all he had to do was to open it and give a jump on to the beanstalk which ran up just like a big ladder. So Jack climbed, and he climbed, and he climbed, and he climbed, and he climbed, and he climbed and he climbed till at last he reached the sky. And when he got there he found a long broad road going as straight as a dart.

So he walked along, and he walked along, and he walked along till he came to a great big tall house, and on the doorstep there was a great big tall woman.

"Good morning, mum," says Jack, quite polite-like. "Could you be so kind as to give me some breakfast?" For he hadn't had anything to eat, you know, the night before, and was as hungry as a hunter.

52

"It's breakfast you want, is it?" says the great big tall woman. "It's breakfast you'll be if you don't move off from here. My man is an ogre and there's nothing he likes better than boys broiled on toast. You'd better be moving on or he'll soon be coming."

"Oh! please mum, do give me something to eat, mum. I've had nothing to eat since yesterday morning, really and truly, mum," says Jack. "I may as well be broiled as die of hunger."

Well, the ogre's wife was not half so bad after all. So she took Jack into the kitchen and gave him a chunk of bread and cheese and a jug of milk. But Jack hadn't half finished these when thump! thump! thump! the whole house began to tremble with the noise of someone coming.

"Goodness gracious me! It's my old man," said the ogre's wife, "what on earth shall I do? Come along quick and jump in here." And she bundled Jack into a chest just as the ogre came in.

He was a big one, to be sure. At his belt he had three calves strung up by the heels, and he unhooked them and threw them down on the table and said: "Here, wife, broil me a couple of these for breakfast. Ah! what's this I smell?

*Fee-fi-fo-fum,*
*I smell the blood of an Englishman.*
*Be he alive, or be he dead*
*I'll have his bones to grind my bread."*

"Nonsense, dear," said his wife, "you're dreaming. Or perhaps you smell the scraps of that little boy you liked so much for yesterday's dinner. Here, you go and have a wash and tidy up, and by the time you come back your breakfast'll be ready for you."

So off the ogre went, and Jack was just going to jump out of the chest and run away when the woman told him not to. "Wait till he's asleep," says she; "he always has a doze after breakfast."

Well, the ogre had his breakfast, and after that he goes to a big chest and takes out of it a couple of bags of gold, and down he sits and counts till at last his head began to nod, and he began to snore till the whole house shook again.

Then Jack crept out on tiptoe from his chest, and as he was passing the ogre he took one of the bags of gold under his arm, and off he pelters till he came to the beanstalk, and then he threw down the bag of gold, which of course fell into his mother's garden, and then he climbed down, and climbed down till at last he got home and told his mother and showed her the gold and said, "Well mother, wasn't I right about the beans? They are really magical, you see."

So they lived on the bag of gold for some time, but at last they came to the end of it, and Jack made up his mind to try his luck once more up at the top of the beanstalk. So one fine morning he rose up early, and got on to the beanstalk, and he climbed, and he climbed, and he climbed, and he climbed, and he climbed, and he climbed till at last he came out on to the road again and up to the great big tall house he had been to before. There, sure enough, was the great big tall woman a-standing on the doorstep.

"Good morning, mum," says Jack, as bold as brass, "could you be so good as to give me something to eat?"

"Go away, my boy," said the big tall woman, "or else my man will eat you up for breakfast. But aren't you the youngster who came here once before? Do you know, that very day, my man missed one of his bags of gold."

"That's strange, mum," said Jack, "I dare say I could tell you something about that; but I'm so hungry I can't speak till I've had something to eat."

Well, the big tall woman was so curious that she took him in and gave him something to eat. But he had scarcely begun munching it as slowly as he could when thump! thump! thump! they heard the giant's footstep, and his wife hid Jack away in the chest.

All happened as it did before. In came the ogre as he did before, said: "Fee-fi-fo-fum," and had his breakfast off three broiled oxen. Then he said: "Wife, bring me the hen that lays the golden eggs." So she brought it, and the ogre said: "Lay," and it laid an egg all of gold. And then the ogre began to nod his head and to snore till the house shook.

Then Jack crept out of the chest on tiptoe and caught hold of the golden hen and was off before you could say "Jack Robinson." But this time the hen gave a cackle which woke the ogre, and just as Jack got out of the house he heard him calling: "Wife, wife, what have you done with my golden hen?"

And the wife said: "Why, my dear?"

But that was all Jack heard, for he rushed off to the beanstalk and climbed down like a house on fire. And when he got home he showed his mother the wonderful hen, and said, "Lay," to it; and it laid a golden egg every time he said, "Lay."

Well, Jack was not content, and it wasn't very long before he determined to have another try at his luck up there at the top of the beanstalk. So one fine morning, he rose up early and got on to the beanstalk, and he climbed, and he climbed, and he climbed, and he climbed till he got to the top. But this time he knew better than to go straight to the ogre's house. And when he got near it, he waited behind a bush till he saw the ogre's wife come out with a pail to get some water, and then he crept into the house and got into the copper. He hadn't been there long when he heard thump! thump! thump! as before, and in came the ogre and his wife.

"Fee-fi-fo-fum, I smell the blood of an Englishman," cried out the ogre. "I smell him, wife, I smell him."

"Do you, my dearie?" says the ogre's wife. "Then, if it's that little rogue that stole your gold and the hen that laid the golden eggs he's sure to have gotten into the chest." And they both rushed to the chest. But Jack wasn't there, luckily, and the ogre's wife said: "There you are again with your fee-fi-fo-fum. Why of course it's the boy you caught last night that I've just broiled for your breakfast. How forgetful I am, and how careless you are not to know the difference between live and dead after all these years."

So the ogre sat down to the breakfast and ate it, but every now and then he would mutter: "Well, I could have sworn—" and he'd get up and search the larder and the cupboards and everything, only, luckily, he didn't think of the copper.

After breakfast was over, the ogre called out, "Wife, wife, bring me my golden harp." So she brought it and put it on the table before him. Then he said: "Sing!" and the golden harp sang most beautifully. And it went on singing till the ogre fell asleep and commenced to snore like thunder.

Then Jack lifted up the copper-lid very quietly and got down like a mouse and crept on hands and knees till he came to the table when up he crawled, caught hold of the golden harp and dashed with it towards the door. But the harp called out quite loud: "Master! Master!" and the ogre woke up just in time to see Jack running off with his harp.

Jack ran as fast as he could, and the ogre came rushing after and would soon have caught him only Jack had a start and dodged him a bit and knew where he was going. When he got to the beanstalk the ogre was not more than twenty yards away when suddenly he saw Jack disappear like, and when he came to the end of the road he saw Jack underneath climbing down for dear life. Well, the ogre didn't like trusting himself to such a ladder, and he stood and waited; so Jack got another start. But just then the harp cried out: "Master! Master!" and the ogre swung himself down on to the beanstalk, which shook with his weight. Down climbs Jack, and after him climbed the ogre. By this time Jack had climbed down, and climbed down, and climbed down till he was very nearly home. So he called out: "Mother! Mother! bring me an axe; bring me an axe." And his mother came rushing out with the axe in her hand, but when she came to the beanstalk she stood stock still with fright, for there she saw the ogre with his legs just through the clouds.

But Jack jumped down and got hold of the axe and gave a chop at the beanstalk which cut it half in two. The ogre felt the beanstalk shake and quiver, so he stopped to see what was the matter. Then Jack gave another chop with the axe, and the beanstalk was cut in two and began to topple over. Then the ogre fell down and broke his crown, and the beanstalk came toppling after.

Then Jack showed his mother his golden harp, and what with showing that and selling the golden eggs Jack and his mother became very rich, and he married a great princess, and they lived happy ever after.

# Jabberwocky

BY LEWIS CARROLL

'Twas brillig, and the slithy toves
    Did gyre and gimble in the wabe;
All mimsy were the borogoves,
    And the mome raths outgrabe.

"Beware the Jabberwock, my son!
    The jaws that bite, the claws that catch!
Beware the Jubjub bird, and shun
    The frumious Bandersnatch!"

He took his vorpal sword in hand:
    Long time the manxome foe he sought—
So rested he by the Tumtum tree,
    And stood awhile in thought.

And as in uffish thought he stood,
    The Jabberwock, with eyes of flame,
Came whiffling through the tulgey wood,
    And burbled as it came!

One, two! One, two! And through and through
    The vorpal blade went snicker-snack!
He left it dead, and with its head
    He went galumphing back.

"And hast thou slain the Jabberwock?
    Come to my arms, my beamish boy!
O frabjous day! Callooh! Callay!"
    He chortled in his joy.

'Twas brillig, and the slithy toves
    Did gyre and gimble in the wabe;
All mimsy were the borogoves,
    And the mome raths outgrabe.

# The Gingerbread Boy

## AUTHOR UNKNOWN

Now you shall hear a story that somebody's great-great-grandmother told a little girl ever so many years ago:

There was once a little old man and a little old woman, who lived in a little old house in the edge of a wood. They would have been a very happy old couple but for one thing—they had no little child, and they

wished for one very much. One day, when the little old woman was baking gingerbread, she cut a cake in the shape of a little boy, and put it into the oven.

Presently, she went to the oven to see if it was baked. As soon as the oven door was opened, the little gingerbread boy jumped out, and began to run away as fast as he could go.

65

The little old woman called her husband, and they both ran after him. But they could not catch him. And soon the gingerbread boy came to a barn full of threshers. He called out to them as he went by, saying:

"*I've run away from a little old woman,*
*A little old man,*
*And I can run away from you, I can!*"

Then the barn full of threshers set out to run after him. But, though they ran fast, they could not catch him. And he ran on till he came to a field full of mowers. He called out to them:

"*I've run away from a little old woman,*
*A little old man,*
*A barn full of threshers,*
*And I can run away from you, I can!*"

Then the mowers began to run after him, but they couldn't catch him. And he ran on till he came to a cow. He called out to her:

"*I've run away from a little old woman,*
*A little old man,*
*A barn full of threshers,*
*A field full of mowers,*
*And I can run away from you, I can!*"

But, though the cow started at once, she couldn't catch him. And soon he came to a pig. He called out to the pig:

"*I've run away from a little old woman,*
*A little old man,*
*A barn full of threshers,*
*A field full of mowers,*
*A cow,*
*And I can run away from you, I can!*"

But the pig ran, and couldn't catch him. And he ran till he came across a fox, and to him he called out:

"*I've run away from a little old woman,*
        *A little old man,*
        *A barn full of threshers,*
        *A field full of mowers,*
        *A cow and a pig,*
    *And I can run away from you, I can!*"

Then the fox set out to run. Now foxes can run very fast, and so the fox soon caught the gingerbread boy and began to eat him up.

70

Presently the gingerbread boy said: "Oh, dear! I'm quarter gone!"
and then: "Oh, I'm half gone!" And soon: "I'm three-quarters gone!" And
at last: "I'm all gone!" and never spoke again.

# *From* A Child's Garden of Verses

BY ROBERT LOUIS STEVENSON

### RAIN

The rain is raining all around,
    It falls on field and tree,
It rains on the umbrellas here,
    And on the ships at sea.


### MY SHADOW

I have a little shadow that goes in and out with me,
And what can be the use of him is more than I can see.
He is very, very like me from the heels up to the head;
And I see him jump before me, when I jump into my bed.

The funniest thing about him is the way he likes to grow—
Not at all like proper children, which is always very slow;
For he sometimes shoots up taller like an india-rubber ball,
And he sometimes gets so little that there's none of him at all.

He hasn't got a notion of how children ought to play,
And can only make a fool of me in every sort of way.
He stays so close beside me, he's a coward you can see;
I'd think shame to stick to nursie as that shadow sticks to me!

One morning, very early, before the sun was up,
I rose and found the shining dew on every buttercup;
But my lazy little shadow, like an errant sleepyhead,
Had stayed at home behind me and was fast asleep in bed.

72

### THE SWING

How do you like to go up in a swing,
  Up in the air so blue?
Oh, I do think it the pleasantest thing
  Ever a child can do!

Up in the air and over the wall,
  Till I can see so wide,
Rivers and trees and cattle and all
  Over the countryside—

Till I look down on the garden green,
  Down on the roof so brown—
Up in the air I go flying again,
  Up in the air and down!

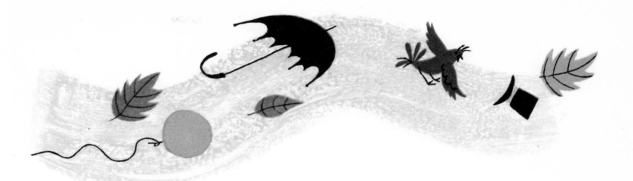

### The Wind

I saw you toss the kites on high
And blow the birds about the sky;
And all around I heard you pass,
Like ladies' skirts across the grass—
  O wind, a-blowing all day long,
  O wind, that sings so loud a song!

I saw the different things you did,
But always you yourself you hid.
I felt you push, I heard you call,
I could not see yourself at all—
  O wind, a-blowing all day long,
  O wind, that sings so loud a song!

O you that are so strong and cold,
O blower, are you young or old?
Are you a beast of field and tree,
Or just a stronger child than me?
  O wind, a-blowing all day long,
  O wind, that sings so loud a song!

### THE LAND OF COUNTERPANE

When I was sick and lay a-bed,
I had two pillows at my head,
And all my toys beside me lay
To keep me happy all the day.

And sometimes for an hour or so
I watched my leaden soldiers go,
With different uniforms and drills,
Among the bedclothes, through the hills;

And sometimes sent my ships in fleets
All up and down among the sheets;
Or brought my trees and houses out,
And planted cities all about.

I was the giant great and still
That sits upon the pillow-hill,
And sees before him, dale and plain,
The pleasant land of counterpane.

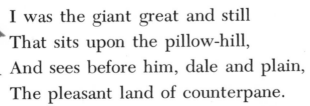

## The Land of Story-Books

At evening when the lamp is lit,
Around the fire my parents sit;
They sit at home and talk and sing,
And do not play at anything.

Now, with my little gun, I crawl
All in the dark along the wall,
And follow round the forest track
Away behind the sofa back.

There, in the night, where none can spy,
All in my hunter's camp I lie,
And play at books that I have read
Till it is time to go to bed.

These are the hills; these are the woods;
These are my starry solitudes;
And there the river by whose brink
The roaring lions come to drink.

I see the others far away
As if in firelit camp they lay,
And I, like. to an Indian scout,
Around their party prowled about.

So, when my nurse comes in for me,
Home I return across the sea,
And go to bed with backward looks
At my dear land of Story-books.

### TIME TO RISE

A birdie with a yellow bill
Hopped upon the window sill,
Cocked his shining eye and said:
"Ain't you 'shamed, you sleepy-head!"


### HAPPY THOUGHT

The world is so full of a number of things,
I'm sure we should all be as happy as kings.

# The Pied Piper

RETOLD BY LOUIS UNTERMEYER

Hamelin, a little German town in the duchy of Brunswick, was overrun by rats. They were so fierce and so numerous that they attacked the cats and drove the dogs out of the city. All kinds of traps were laid, but the rats just flipped them about. The creatures swarmed through the streets, broke into the houses, filled the attics, invaded the kitchens, sprang on the tables, and raced through the bedrooms. They were everywhere.

The townspeople complained bitterly. "What kind of a mayor have we got!" they said. "He should not allow such a thing to happen! He sits in his elegant office, gazes out the window, and does nothing about it!"

The mayor summoned his councillors, but they were no help. Day after day they met, but nothing they thought up had the slightest effect on the plague of rats. It grew worse every hour.

One summer morning—the records give the year as 1376—a tall, odd-looking stranger entered Hamelin and came straight to the town hall.

The stranger advanced to the council table and spoke directly to the mayor.

"I hear," he said, "that you are troubled with rats. I can help you, for I happen to be a rat-catcher. By means of a certain power—call it music or call it magic—I can rid your town of the pests that are such a plague to you. People call me the Pied Piper."

The mayor looked up at the man and noticed that at the end of the stranger's red and yellow scarf there hung a small pipe, and the stranger's fingers kept twitching as though they wanted to be playing on it.

"Yes," continued the strange figure, "I have freed many cities of rats, as well as gnats and bats. I will do the same for you—" he paused for a moment and coughed gently, "only you will have to pay me a thousand guilders."

"A thousand guilders?" echoed the mayor. "Make it fifty thousand! If you can really clear Hamelin of rats, it will be well worth it!"

The piper stepped into the street and played a shrill tune on his pipe. As he played, rats came tumbling out of the houses. It was as if an army were on the run, murmuring and muttering. The muttering grew to a grumbling, the grumbling to a rumbling. The air was filled with a mighty humming, a humming that changed to drumming.

And still the rats kept coming. Great rats, small rats, lean rats, tall rats, young rats, old rats, big rats, bold rats, rats of every size and color. They followed the piper wherever he went. Still playing, he led them to the river Weser and waded in. Into the river went the rats—and there every single rat drowned.

The piper returned to the city hall and asked politely for his thousand guilders. The mayor looked blank.

"You must be joking," said the mayor. "Surely you wouldn't expect anyone to pay such a huge sum of money for getting rid of a few rats. Besides, the river did most of the work for you. A thousand guilders? Don't be silly. Come, take fifty."

The piper's face grew dark. "I don't drive bargains," he said. "I want the full payment agreed upon. If not, you will be sorry that you didn't keep your promise. See, I still have my pipe. And if you force me, I can play a different tune."

"What!" exclaimed the mayor angrily. "You dare to threaten me! The mayor of Hamelin is not to be insulted by a fool in crazy clothes! Get out! Do your worst! Blow on your pipe until you burst!"

The piper did not say another word. He left the council room and stepped out into the street. Putting his lips to the pipe, he blew again. This time the sound was anything but shrill. It was sweet and low, a dreamy tune, full of delightful turns and twists, gentle and at the same time gay, promising all manner of marvelous things.

As he played, there came a sound of little hands clapping and feet pattering, of small voices chattering, like chicks in a barnyard when corn and grain are scattering. Out of the houses came boys and girls, flocking to the piper, tripping and skipping, following after the magic music with shouting and laughter.

People looked on in amazement. The mayor cried "Stop!" But the children paid no attention to anything or anyone except the piper. Singing and dancing, they followed him out of town.

This time the piper did not guide them toward the river but toward the hills. When they came to the Koppelberg, a side of the mountain opened as though it were a door and all the children—one hundred and thirty of them—trooped inside. Then the hill closed up. Not one of these boys or girls was ever seen again.

It would never have been known what the piper's music promised, what was to be seen inside the hill, had it not been for one lame boy. He never tired of saying how dull it was in Hamelin without his playmates nor of telling what he remembered.

"Because of my lame foot," he said, "I was a little behind the others. We were all gay as on a holiday. We were all looking forward to the place the piper—I mean the piper's music—told us about. It was a land where all things were beautiful and all people were good. A dozen rivers flowed there, each with a different sweet flavor. The flowers were larger and lovelier than anywhere else on earth. The sparrows were not dull brown as they are here, but brighter than peacocks. Dogs ran faster than deer and never barked. Bees had lost their sting. Horses were born with eagles' wings. No one was ever sad or sick, and anyone who came to the place with anything wrong—like a lame foot—was instantly cured. Just as I was about to catch up with the other children, the door in the side of the mountain closed, the music stopped, and I was left on the Koppelberg, alone."

All of this happened (or was believed to have happened) centuries ago. But still, they say, no one is allowed to play the pipe in Hamelin. Besides, they say that in Transylvania there lives a strange group who wear outlandish garments of red and yellow, and have names something like those of the families that once lived in Hamelin. Not one of them, they say, ever breaks a promise.

# The Real Princess

### BY HANS CHRISTIAN ANDERSEN

There was once a Prince who wished to marry a Princess; but then she must be a real Princess. He traveled all over the world in hopes of finding such a one; but there was always something wrong. Princesses he found in plenty; but he could not make up his mind that they were real Princesses, for now one thing, now another, seemed to him not quite right about them. At last he went back to his palace quite downcast, because he wished so much to have a real Princess for his wife, and he had not been able to find one.

One evening a fearful tempest arose. It thundered and lightninged, and the rain came down in torrents. Besides, it was as dark as pitch. All at once there was a violent knocking at the door, and the old King, the Prince's father, went out himself to open it.

It was a Princess who was standing outside. What with the rain and the wind, she was in a sad state; the water trickled from her hair, and her clothes clung to her body. She said she was a real Princess.

"Ah, we shall soon see about that!" thought the old Queen-mother. She gave no hint whatever of what she was going to do, but went quietly into the bedroom, took all the bed-clothes off the bed, and put three little peas on the bedstead. Then she laid twenty mattresses one upon another over the three peas, and put twenty feather-beds over the mattresses.

Upon this bed the Princess was to pass the night.

The next morning she was asked how she had slept. "Oh, very badly indeed!" she replied. "I have scarcely closed my eyes the whole night through. I do not know what was in my bed, but I had something hard under me, and am all over black and blue. It has hurt me so much!"

Now it was plain that this must be a real Princess, since she had been able to feel the three little peas through the twenty mattresses and twenty feather-beds. None but a real Princess could have had such a delicate sense of feeling.

So the Prince made her his wife, being now convinced that he had found a real Princess. The three peas were, however, put into the royal museum, where they are still to be seen, if they have not been stolen.

Notice that this is a true story.

# The Three Billy-Goats Gruff

### RETOLD BY PETER CHRISTIAN ASBJORNSEN

Once on a time there were three Billy-Goats who were to go up to the hillside to make themselves fat, and the family name of the three goats was "Gruff."

On the way up was a bridge, over a burn they had to cross; and under the bridge lived a great ugly Troll, with eyes as big as saucers and a nose as long as a poker.

First of all came the youngest Billy-Goat Gruff to cross the bridge.

"Trip, trap! Trip, trap!" went the bridge.

"WHO'S THAT tripping over my bridge?" roared the Troll.

"Oh! it is only I, the tiniest Billy-Goat Gruff, and I'm going up to the hillside to make myself fat," said the Billy-Goat, with such a small voice.

"Now, I'm coming to gobble you up," said the Troll.

"Oh, no! pray don't take me. I'm too little, that I am," said the Billy-Goat. "Wait a bit till the second Billy-Goat Gruff comes; he's much bigger."

"Well! be off with you," said the Troll.

A little while after came the second Billy-Goat Gruff to cross the bridge.

"Trip, trap! Trip, trap! Trip, trap!" went the bridge.

"WHO'S THAT tripping over my bridge?" roared the Troll.

"Oh! it's the second Billy-Goat Gruff, and I'm going up to the hillside to make myself fat," said the Billy-Goat, who hadn't such a small voice.

"Now, I'm coming to gobble you up," said the Troll.

"Oh, no! don't take me. Wait a little till the big Billy-Goat Gruff comes; he's much bigger."

"Very well! be off with you," said the Troll.

But just then up came the big Billy-Goat Gruff.

"*Trip, trap! Trip, trap! Trip, trap!*" went the bridge, for the Billy-Goat was so heavy that the bridge creaked and groaned under him.

"WHO'S THAT tramping over my bridge?" roared the Troll.

"It's I! THE BIG BILLY-GOAT GRUFF," said the Billy-Goat, who had a big hoarse voice of his own.

"Now, I'm coming to gobble you up," roared the Troll.

"Well, come along! I've got two spears,
And I'll poke your eyeballs out at your ears,
I've got besides two curling-stones,
And I'll crush you to bits, body and bones."

That was what the big Billy-Goat said. So he flew at the Troll and poked his eyes out with his horns, and crushed him to bits, body and bones, and tossed him out into the burn, and after that he went up to the hillside. There the Billy-Goats got so fat they were scarcely able to walk home again; and if the fat hasn't fallen off them, why they're still fat. And so—

       "Snip, snap, snout,
         This tale's told out."

# The Story of the Three Bears

**RETOLD BY FLORA ANNIE STEEL**

Once upon a time there were three Bears, who lived together in a house of their own, in a wood. One of them was a Little Wee Bear, and one was a Middle-sized Bear, and the other was a Great Big Bear. They had each a bowl for their porridge: a little bowl for the Little Wee Bear; and a middle-sized bowl for the Middle-sized Bear; and a great bowl for the Great Big Bear. And they had each a chair to sit in:

a little chair for the Little Wee Bear; and a middle-sized chair for the Middle-sized Bear; and a great chair for the Great Big Bear. And they had each a bed to sleep in: a little bed for the Little Wee Bear; and a middle-sized bed for the Middle-sized Bear; and a great bed for the Great Big Bear.

One day, after they had made the porridge for their breakfast and poured it into their porridge-bowls, they walked out into the wood while the porridge was cooling that they might not burn their mouths by beginning too soon, for they were polite, well-brought-up Bears. And while they were away, a little girl called Goldilocks, who lived at the other side of the wood and had been sent on an errand by her mother,

passed by the house and looked in at the window. And then she peeped in at the keyhole, for she was not at all a well-brought-up little girl. Then seeing nobody in the house she lifted the latch. The door was not fastened, because the Bears were good Bears, who did nobody any harm and never suspected that anybody would harm them. So Goldilocks opened the door and went in; and well pleased was she when she saw the porridge on the table. If she had been a well-brought-up little girl she would have waited till the Bears came home, and then, perhaps, they would have asked her to breakfast; for they were good Bears—a little rough or so, as the manner of Bears is, but for all that very good-natured and hospitable. But she was an impudent, rude little girl, and so she set about helping herself.

First she tasted the porridge of the Great Big Bear, and that was too hot for her. Next she tasted the porridge of the Middle-sized Bear, but that was too cold for her. And then she went to the porridge of the Little

Wee Bear, and tasted it, and that was neither too hot nor too cold, but just right, and she liked it so well, that she ate it all up, every bit!

Then Goldilocks, who was tired, for she had been catching butterflies instead of running on her errand, sate down in the chair of the Great Big Bear, but that was too hard for her. And then she sate down in the chair of the Middle-sized Bear, and that was too soft for her. But when she sate down in the chair of the Little Wee Bear, that was neither too hard, nor too soft, but just right. So she seated herself in it, and there she sate till the bottom of the chair came out, and down she came, plump upon the ground; and that made her very cross, for she was a bad-tempered little girl.

Now, being determined to rest, Goldilocks went upstairs into the bedchamber in which the three Bears slept. And first she lay down upon the bed of the Great Big Bear, but that was too high at the head for her. And next she lay down upon the bed of the Middle-sized Bear, and

that was too high at the foot for her. And then she lay down upon the bed of the Little Wee Bear, and that was neither too high at the head, nor at the foot, but just right. So she covered herself up comfortably, and lay there till she fell fast asleep.

By this time the Three Bears thought their porridge would be cool enough for them to eat it properly; so they came home to breakfast. Now careless Goldilocks had left the spoon of the Great Big Bear standing in his porridge.

"SOMEBODY HAS BEEN AT MY PORRIDGE!" said the Great Big Bear in his great, rough, gruff voice.

Then the Middle-sized Bear looked at her porridge and saw the spoon was standing in it too.

"*Somebody Has Been At My Porridge!*" said the Middle-sized Bear in her middle-sized voice.

Then the Little Wee Bear looked at his, and there was the spoon in the porridge-bowl, but the porridge was all gone!

"Somebody has been at my porridge, and has eaten it all up!" said the Little Wee Bear in his little wee voice.

Upon this the Three Bears, seeing that someone had entered their house, and eaten up the Little Wee Bear's breakfast, began to look about them. Now the careless Goldilocks had not put the hard cushion straight when she rose from the chair of the Great Big Bear.

"SOMEBODY HAS BEEN SITTING IN MY CHAIR!" said the Great Big Bear in his great, rough, gruff voice.

And the careless Goldilocks had squatted down the soft cushion of the Middle-sized Bear.

"*Somebody Has Been Sitting In My Chair!*" said the Middle-sized Bear in her middle-sized voice.

"Somebody has been sitting in my chair, and has sate the bottom through!" said the Little Wee Bear in his little wee voice.

Then the Three Bears thought they had better make further search in case it was a burglar; so they went up stairs into their bedchamber. Now Goldilocks had pulled the Great Big Bear's pillow out of its place.

"SOMEBODY HAS BEEN LYING IN MY BED!" said the Great Big Bear in his great, rough, gruff voice.

98

And Goldilocks had pulled the bolster of the Middle-sized Bear out of its place.

"*Somebody Has Been Lying In My Bed!*" said the Middle-sized Bear in her middle-sized voice.

But when the Little Wee Bear came to look at his bed, there was the bolster in its place!

And the pillow was in its place. And upon the pillow—?

There was Goldilocks' yellow head—which was not in its place, for she had no business there.

"Somebody has been lying in my bed,—and here she is still!" said the Little Wee Bear in his little wee voice.

Now Goldilocks had heard in her sleep the great, rough, gruff voice of the Great Big Bear; but she was so fast asleep that it was no more to her than the roaring of wind, or the rumbling of thunder. And she had heard the middle-sized voice of the Middle-sized Bear, but it was only as if she had heard someone speaking in a dream. But when she heard the little wee voice of the Little Wee Bear, it was so sharp and so shrill that it awakened her at once. Up she started, and when she saw the Three Bears on one side of the bed, she tumbled herself out at the other and ran to the window. Now the window was open, because the Bears, like good, tidy Bears, as they were, always opened their bed-chamber window when they got up in the morning. So naughty, frightened little Goldilocks jumped; and whether she broke her neck in the fall or ran into the wood and was lost there or found her way out of the wood and got whipped for being a bad girl and playing truant no one can say. But the Three Bears never saw anything more of her!

*Here is a story about a mouse and a cat.*
*In this story, the cat has been bought to*
*get rid of the rats which*
*seem to be doing damage to the church.*
*The ferocious rats turn out to be*
*one small mouse who writes poetry,*
*and the cat turns out to be a kitten*
*who is a poetry-lover.*

# Peter Churchmouse

## BY MARGOT AUSTIN

Up jumped Peter!
S-N-A-P! went the rat-trap!
Poor little Peter Churchmouse raised his eyebrows the way he always did when he made a poem,

> "I wish the cheese I ate
> Were on a plate
> That wouldn't snap at me
> Because I DON'T LIKE IT!"

Then Peter sat right down on the big wooden rat-trap and ate his cheese. Every last bit.

100

"Now," said Peter, "I shall bite another big hole in something so that Parson Pease-Porridge will put more cheese on the rat-trap for tomorrow."

So Peter ate a great big hole in the red felt that lined Parson Pease-Porridge's best collection basket.

"There," said Peter, "Parson Pease-Porridge will be *sure* to notice that!"

"I'll be twitched," said Parson Pease-Porridge next morning when he saw the great big hole that Peter had made in the best collection basket.

"These holes will be the ruination of me. I must do something drastic! I'll show these rats—I'll get a *cat!!*"

"Oh-h-h," said Peter Churchmouse. "Oh-h-h, poor me!"

Then Peter Churchmouse raised his eyebrows the way he always did when he thought of a poem,

"I believe I heard
That terrible word
I'm scared to tell it
So I'll only spell it—
C-A-T!"

Next day Peter looked for cheese on the rat-trap as usual.

But the rat-trap was gone and in its place was a bowl of milk. And beside the bowl of milk was Gabriel.

"Hello," said Peter stepping bravely from behind the organ, "I'm afraid of cats. Are you a cat?"

"Who? Me?" said Gabriel sitting up. "I'm not a cat. I'm a kitten and my name's Gabriel. Are you a rat?"

"Of course not," said Peter. "I'm a poor Churchmouse and my name is Peter."

"Hello, Peter," said Gabriel. "I'm to scare the rats away. The rats who've been eating big holes in things. Do you know how to scare rats?"

"No I don't," said Peter. "And if I did it wouldn't help you because there aren't any rats here at all. There's only poor me. I pretend I'm rats. *I* bite the great big holes in everything!"

"You don't!" said Gabriel.

"I do," said Peter. "Once I even ate a hymn book. It tasted awful."

"For pity's sake," said Gabriel in a shocked voice. "Cover and all?"

"Cover and all," said Peter. "And I didn't like to do it."

"Then why *did* you do it?" asked Gabriel.

"Because I was hungry," said Peter. "I'm *always* hungry!"

"How sad for you," said Gabriel. "Parson Pease-Porridge gives *me* lots to eat."

"That's because you're a big kitten and he can see you," cried poor Peter. "But I'm a little mouse and he can't see me at all. He's too short-sighted! He doesn't even know I live here. And now that you've come even the rat-trap is gone. All I ever got to eat was the cheese on the rat-trap and I wouldn't have got that if Parson Pease-Porridge didn't think I was the rats that make the holes *I* bite in things. Fuss, fuss, fuss. Oh, I don't like it!"

"How very sad," said Gabriel. "How very, very sad."

"Sad indeed," said Peter, "I even make poems about it."

"I'd like to hear one, please," said Gabriel.

"Gladly," said Peter, raising his eyebrows. "One goes like this—

Snap, whack, bang,
Goes the rat-trap bang,
Goes snap bang,
Goes whack bang,
Fuss, fuss, fuss!"

"It's a beautful poem," said Gabriel admiringly. "I could listen and listen and listen."

"Thank you kindly," said Peter.

"Maybe I can help you think of a way to let Parson Pease-Porridge know he has a poor hungry Churchmouse," said Gabriel. "So you'll get lots to eat like I do."

"But how?" said Peter.

"I really don't know," said Gabriel. "I'll think very hard."

"Please do," said Peter. "Think hard while I have a lick of your milk."

So Peter played hide-behind-the-hymn-book on the shelf where the hymn books were kept. And Gabriel played chew-the-toe with Parson Pease-Porridge's old black slipper. And they both played slide-up-and-down-the-pew-bench.

And all the while Peter longed and longed for cheese. And all the while Gabriel thought and thought about how he could help poor Peter. But Gabriel couldn't think of a single way.

"Listen, Gabriel," said Peter at last.

"I am," said Gabriel. "I'm listening."

"That's fine," said Peter, "Because *I* have an idea about how I can get Parson Pease-Porridge to notice me."

"And get some cheese," added Gabriel.

"Well," said Peter. "I've heard Parson Pease-Porridge

say that little children who drink lots of milk grow up to be big children, and you're a big kitten so it must be because you drink lots of milk. So *maybe* if I drink lots of milk I'll grow so big that Parson Pease-Porridge will be able to see me!"

"I *am* a big kitten," admitted Gabriel. "So that must be the reason. Help yourself to some more of my milk."

"Thank you," said Peter between licks, "I much prefer cheese but I'll take anything, even milk, if only Parson Pease-Porridge will notice me!"

"I'll be twitched," remarked Parson Pease-Porridge. "I never knew a kitten to drink so much milk!"

For Peter drank and drank and drank Gabriel's milk every day. And every day he asked Gabriel if he had grown any bigger. And every day he looked in the mirror over the organ to see if he looked any bigger. And every day Gabriel measured him alongside Parson Pease-Porridge's ink bottle to see if he stretched any bigger—but he didn't. Not one bit.

"Except," said Gabriel, "your waist is nearly as round as the ink bottle."

"It's no use," said poor Peter, "no use at all."

"Make a poem about it," said Gabriel.

"Very well," said Peter, lifting his eyebrows—

> "Drink, drink, drink,
> To make me bigger;
> But all I do
> Is lose my figure.
> Fuss, fuss, fuss!"

"How beautiful," said Gabriel. "I could listen and listen."

Peter stopped dancing on the black notes of the organ and looked over the edge of the keyboard at Gabriel.

"Gabriel, do you know what?" asked Peter.

Gabriel stopped sharpening his nails on the organ's green carpet pedals and looked up at Peter.

"I don't," said Gabriel.

"I have another idea, that's what!" said Peter. "About how I can get Parson Pease-Porridge to notice me."

"And get some cheese," added Gabriel.

"If," said Peter, waving his arms, "Parson Pease-Porridge saw my nice red knitted bed he'd know it was much too small for rats to sleep in. So he'd know straight away that a little Churchmouse slept in it. Wouldn't he?"

"Quite true," agreed Gabriel. "And it's such a beautiful bed, too."

"It *is* a nice bed," said Peter. "We'll put it beside his black leather book so he'll be sure to see it."

"We'll do it right now," said Gabriel, "because I've heard Parson Pease-Porridge say 'never put off till tomorrow what you can do right now.'"

So Peter and Gabriel laid the red knitted bed right beside the big black leather book.

"There," said Peter, "Parson Pease-Porridge will be *sure* to notice that!"

"I'll be twitched," said Parson Pease-Porridge when he saw Peter's knitted bed beside his black leather book.

"How in the world did my old red mitten get here? I've been hunting for that good red mitten for ages. Hemmmp! I'm a forgetful old man! So I'll just put this mitten in my pocket so I won't lose it again, Hemp, hemp-p-p!"

And away went Parson Pease-Porridge with Peter's bed.

"How very, very sad," said Gabriel. "Now your bed's gone."

"It's the only bed I had," said poor little Peter. "The only bed I *ever* had."

"You *should* make a poem about it," encouraged Gabriel.

"I will," said Peter lifting his eyebrows—

"I had a bed,
My bed was red.
Now it's gone,
I have no place to rest my head.
It's gone—my lovely bed!"

"It's a beautiful poem," said Gabriel. "It's so sad, I could listen and listen and listen."

"Peter, do you know what?" asked Gabriel.

"I do not," said Peter who was sniffing the flowers that stood on Parson Pease-Porridge's desk.

"I have an idea," answered Gabriel, "that will be *sure* to get Parson Pease-Porridge to notice you."

"So I'll get some cheese," said Peter. "Hurry up and tell me."

"It's this," said Gabriel. "If you stood right under Parson Pease-Porridge's nose he'd have to see you. Wouldn't he?"

"True," said Peter. "But how *can* I stand right under Parson Pease-Porridge's nose? He's much too tall."

"It's really quite simple," said Gabriel. "When Parson Pease-Porridge sits at his desk to read his big black book it's right under his nose. So if you jump out of those flowers, plop, onto the big black book you'll be right under his nose, too. Then if you'll stand very still he'll be sure to notice you."

"True, true," said Peter. "I'll climb into the flowers right now."

"Do hurry," whispered Gabriel. "Parson Pease-Porridge is coming!"

"Hum-mp," said Parson Pease-Porridge sitting down at his desk.

"Hemp, hem-mmp," said Parson Pease-Porridge opening his big black leather book.

"Now," whispered Peter to himself. "Now is the time!"

So plop, jumped Peter, plump in the middle. Right under Parson Pease-Porridge's nose!

"And *now*," said Peter to himself, "Parson Pease-Porridge will be *sure* to notice me."

"I'll be twitched," said Parson Pease-Porridge, pushing up his spectacles. "What's this? Oh, I'm a bothered old man.

"I'll be twitched," said Parson Pease-Porridge, pushing his spectacles down again. "I see a grey spot before my eyes!

"I must have my glasses changed," said he, closing his big book with a terrible—B—A—N—G!

"Oh-h-h," gasped Peter. "Oh-h, poor me."

"He thought you were a grey spot," said Gabriel.

"I might have been," said Peter.

"Very true," said Gabriel. "How awful!"

"I shall make a poem about it," said Peter raising his eyebrows—

"I jumped quick
When the book closed whang.
I learned the trick
On the rat-trap bang.
Fuss, fuss, fuss!"

"Very lovely," sighed Gabriel. "I could listen and listen."

"I have another idea," said Gabriel.

"About how I can get Parson Pease-Porridge to notice me so I'll get cheese?" asked Peter.

"That's right," said Gabriel.

"Then please stop playing jump-over-the-pew-bench," said Peter, "because I'm listening."

"It's this," said Gabriel. "I'll spill Parson Pease-Porridge's ink bottle. Then you can walk in the ink and make foot-prints on his big white blotter, and when he sees your little foot-prints he'll know you're a little Churchmouse."

"Then I'll get cheese," said Peter. "Cheese!"

"Quite true," said Gabriel. "Follow me."

So up they jumped onto Parson Pease-Porridge's desk. Gabriel gave the ink bottle a big push. Over it went and out came the ink.

"Now," said Gabriel. "Make some tracks."

"I will," said Peter running right through the ink and right onto Parson Pease-Porridge's clean white blotter. And he went round and round and round.

"Stop, Peter!" cried Gabriel. "Stop!"

"Why?" asked Peter.

"Because," cried Gabriel, "look what's happening!"

For every step poor Peter took on the blotter was spreading bigger and bigger.

"Don't make more prints. Parson Pease-Porridge will think I've done it," cried Gabriel. "Quick! Dry your feet on something!"

"I'll dry my feet here," said Peter, jumping from the blotter to the sermon that Parson Pease-Porridge had finished writing that very morning.

"Hurry, hurry," cried Gabriel. "Here comes Parson Pease-Porridge. We'd better go!"

"Fuss, fuss, fuss," said Peter wiping his feet very hard all along the bottom of Parson Pease-Porridge's sermon.

"I'll be twitched," said Parson Pease-Porridge, "Gabriel has spilled my ink! Tut, tut, look at his big tracks on my blotter!

"Tut, tut, *tut*," said Parson Pease-Porridge looking from the blotter to his sermon, "I'm a bothered old man. It seems I've made foot-notes on the bottom of my sermon, but I can't seem to read them. Hem-mp! That settles it. I *must* have my glasses changed this *very* day.

"A pretty pass!" said Parson Pease-Porridge as he hurried away. "Can't even read my *own* foot-notes!"

"It's no use," said Peter. "Parson Pease-Porridge will never notice me. Never."

"And you'll never get any cheese," added Gabriel.

"But I *must* have cheese," cried Peter.

"How sad for you," said Gabriel. "Make a poem about it."

"I shall," said Peter lifting his eyebrows—

"Oh, please, please,
I want cheese.
I'm sad, sad,
I wish I had
Cheese, Cheese, CHEESE!"

"Lovely," said Gabriel. "I could listen and listen."

"Gabriel," said Peter, "I'm going to bite a hole in something!"

"Oh, do!" encouraged Gabriel. "Do bite something!"

"I will," said Peter. "I'll bite a hole right through the middle of Parson Pease-Porridge's sermon! Then he'll notice me!"

So Peter began to bite and bite right through the middle of Parson Pease-Porridge's sermon.

"Oh my, it's the biggest hole I've ever seen," admired Gabriel, when Peter had finished.

"It's the biggest hole I ever bit," said Peter.

The next day Parson Pease-Porridge had a new pair of spectacles that were three times as thick and three times as strong as his old ones.

"Hem-mp," said he. "It's fine to have new spectacles. I can see everything. I believe I'll have a look at my sermon!

"I'll be twitched," cried Parson Pease-Porridge when he saw the *tremendous* hole in the middle of his sermon. "Oh ruination! Oh, I'm a bothered old man!"

And *then* Parson Pease-Porridge looked at the foot-notes that he couldn't read the day before.

"Upon my soul," cried Parson Pease-Porridge. "These are *not* foot-notes, these are foot-prints! Little foot-prints! I have a Churchmouse! Poor little thing he's eaten all these holes to show me he's hungry!"

"Hem-m-mp," said Parson Pease-Porridge. "Owing to this slight accident (here Parson Pease-Porridge looked at the hole in his sermon) I must abandon the text I prepared for today. So I shall speak about KINDNESS instead. KINDNESS to very little animals.

"And now," smiled Parson Pease-Porridge, "never put off till tomorrow what you can do right now!

"I must get CHEESE for my Churchmouse!"

"Oh-h, Gabriel," whispered Peter. "Did you hear that?"

"I did," said Gabriel. "Parson Pease-Porridge has noticed you at last!"

"Oh, poor me," cried Peter. "I'm going to get cheese after all!"

"Quite true," replied Gabriel.

"I'll make a little poem about it," said Peter lifting his eyebrows the way he always did—

"Cheese,
Cheese, cheese,
Cheese, cheese, cheese.
C—H—E—E—S—E!"

"How beautiful," sighed Gabriel. "I could listen and listen and listen."

*The short entertaining history of the two gnomes,*
*Minikin and Manikin, may be a surprise,*
*since it is not very well known.*

# Minikin and Manikin

### RETOLD BY LOUIS UNTERMEYER

Minikin and Manikin were two little gnomes who lived a long, long time ago. One day they went out together to pick raspberries, but as fast as Minikin picked them, Manikin ate them.

Minikin came to look for a stick to make a whip, a whip to beat Manikin, who ate up all his raspberries.

Finally he found a stick. "What news do you bring?" said the stick.

"I do not bring any news because I am too busy looking," said Minikin. "I am looking for a stick, a stick to make a whip, a whip to beat Manikin, who ate up all my raspberries."

"You will not get me," said the stick, "until you get an axe to cut me."

So Minikin came to an axe. "What news do you bring?" said the axe.

"I do not bring any news because I am too busy looking," said Minikin. "I am looking for an axe, an axe to cut a stick, a stick to make a whip, a whip to beat Manikin, who ate up all my raspberries."

"You will not get me," said the axe, "until you get a stone to sharpen me."

So Minikin came to a stone. "What news do you bring?" said the stone.

"I do not bring any news because I am too busy looking," said Minikin. "I am looking for a stone, stone to sharpen axe, axe to cut stick, stick to make whip, whip to beat Manikin, who ate up all my raspberries."

"You will not get me," said the stone, "until you get water to wet me."

So Minikin came to the water. "What news do you bring?" said the water.

"I do not bring any news because I am too busy looking," said Minikin. "I am looking for water, water to wet stone, stone to sharpen axe, axe to cut stick, stick to make whip, whip to beat Manikin, who ate up all my raspberries."

"You will not get me," said the water, "until you get a deer who can swim me."

So Minikin came to a deer. "What news do you bring?" said the deer.

"I do not bring any news because I am too busy looking," said Minikin. "I am looking for a deer, deer to swim water, water to wet stone, stone to sharpen axe, axe to cut stick, stick to make whip, whip to beat Manikin, who ate up all my raspberries."

"You will not get me," said the deer, "until you get a hound who can hunt me."

So Minikin came to a hound. "What news do you bring?" said the hound.

"I do not bring any news because I am too busy looking," said Minikin. "I am looking for a hound, hound to hunt deer, deer to swim water, water to wet stone, stone to sharpen axe, axe to cut stick, stick to make whip, whip to beat Manikin, who ate up all my raspberries."

"You will not get me," said the hound, "until you get a bit of butter to put on my tongue."

So Minikin came to the butter. "What news do you bring?" said the butter.

"I do not bring any news because I am too busy looking," said Minikin. "I am looking for a bit of butter, butter to go on hound's tongue, hound to hunt deer, deer to swim water, water to wet stone, stone to sharpen axe, axe to cut stick, stick to make whip, whip to beat Manikin, who ate up all my raspberries."

"You will not get me," said the butter, "until you find a cat who can scrape me."

So Minikin came to a cat. "What news do you bring?" said the cat.

"I do not bring any news because I am too busy looking," said Minikin. "I am looking for a cat, cat to scrape butter, butter to go on hound's tongue, hound to hunt deer, deer to swim water, water to wet stone, stone to sharpen axe, axe to cut stick, stick to make whip, whip to beat Manikin, who ate up all my raspberries."

"You will not get me," said the cat, "until you get me some milk."

So Minikin came to a cow. "What news do you bring?" said the cow.

"I do not bring any news because I am too busy looking," said Minikin. "I am looking for a cow, cow to give milk, milk to give cat, cat to scrape butter, butter to go on hound's tongue, hound to hunt deer, deer to swim water, water to wet stone, stone to sharpen axe, axe to cut stick, stick to make whip, whip to beat Manikin, who ate up all my raspberries."

"You will not get any milk from me," said the cow, "until you give me some straw from the threshers."

So Minikin came to the threshers. "What news do you bring?" said the threshers.

"I do not bring any news because I am too busy looking," said Minikin. "I am looking for straw, straw to give cow, cow to give milk, milk to give cat, cat to scrape butter, butter to go on hound's tongue, hound to hunt deer, deer to swim water, water to wet stone, stone to sharpen axe, axe to cut stick, stick to make whip, whip to beat Manikin, who ate up all my raspberries."

"You will not get any straw from us," said the threshers, "until you get cake flour for us from the miller over yonder."

So Minikin went to the miller. "What news do you bring?" said the miller.

"I do not bring any news because I am too busy look-

ing," said Minikin. "I am looking for cake flour for the threshers, threshers to give straw, straw to give cow, cow to give milk, milk to give cat, cat to scrape butter, butter to go on hound's tongue, hound to hunt deer, deer to swim water, water to wet stone, stone to sharpen axe, axe to cut stick, stick to make whip, whip to beat Manikin, who ate up all my raspberries."

"You will not get any cake flour from me," said the miller, "until you bring me a sieve full of water from the river."

So Minikin took the sieve and went over to the river. But every time he tried to fill it, the water would run out of the sieve, and he could not carry a drop of it away.

At that moment a crow flew over his head. "Daub! daub!" cawed the crow.

"Blessings on you," said Minikin. "That is good advice."

So he took some clay and the daub that was on the river's brink and he rubbed it over the bottom of the sieve until all the holes were filled. Then the sieve held the water, and he brought the water to the miller, and the miller gave him cake flour, and he gave the cake flour to the threshers, the threshers gave him some straw, he gave the straw to the cow, the cow gave him milk, he gave milk to the cat, the cat scraped the butter, he put the butter on the hound's tongue, the hound hunted the deer, the deer swam the water, the water wet the stone, the stone sharpened the axe, the axe cut the stick, the stick made a whip. But when Minikin had the whip ready to beat Manikin, he found that Manikin had BURST!

*According to the Danish story teller,*
*Hans Christian Andersen,*
*Ole Lukoie was the greatest story teller of all.*
*He was always there when children went to bed.*
*He sprinkled a few drops of milk on*
*the children's eyelids so they could not see him.*
*Then he opened an umbrella with*
*ever-changing beautiful pictures on it—*
*and the pictures changed into dreams....*

# The Mouse's Wedding

### BY HANS CHRISTIAN ANDERSEN

"I tell you what," Ole Lukoie said. "Don't be afraid if I show you a little mouse." He held out a hand with the quaint little creature in it. "It has come to ask you to a wedding. There are two little mice here who are to enter into the state of marriage this very night. They live under the floor of your mother's pantry, which is supposed to be the most charming quarters."

"How can I get through that little mouse hole in the floor?" Hjalmar asked.

"Leave that to me," said Ole Lukoie. "I'll make you small enough." Then he touched Hjalmar with his magic sprinkler. He immediately became shorter and shorter, until at last he was only as tall as your finger. "Now you may borrow the tin soldier's uniform. I think it will just fit you, and uniforms always look well when one is at a party."

"Oh, don't they!" said Hjalmar. Instantly he was dressed like the finest tin soldier.

"If you will be so kind as to sit in your mother's thimble," the mouse said, "I shall consider it an honor to pull you along."

"Will you really go to all that trouble, young lady?" Hjalmar cried.

And in this fashion, off they drove to the mouse's wedding. First they went down a long passage under the floor boards. It was just high enough for them to drive through in the thimble, and the whole passage was lighted with touchwood.

"Doesn't it smell delightful here?" said the mouse. "This whole road has been greased with bacon rinds, and there's nothing better than that."

Now they came to the wedding hall. On the right stood all the little lady mice, whispering and giggling as if they were making fun of each other. On the left stood all the gentlemen mice, twirling their mustaches with their fore-paws. The bridegroom and his bride stood in a hollow cheese rind in the center of the floor, and kissed like mad, in plain view of all the guests. But of course they were engaged, and were to be married immediately.

More and more guests kept crowding in. The mice were

nearly trampling each other to death, and the bridal couple had posted themselves in the doorway, so that no one could come or leave. Like the passage, this whole hall had been greased with bacon rind, and that was the complete banquet. However, for the dessert, a pea was brought in, on which a little mouse of the family had bitten the name of the bridal couple, that is to say the first letter of the name. This was a most unusual touch.

All the mice said it was a charming wedding, and that the conversation was perfect. And then Hjalmar drove home again. He had been in very high society, for all that he had been obliged to make himself very small to fit in the tin soldier's uniform.

# Mother Goose

*Nursery rhymes are so old that nobody knows who invented them...nursery rhymes and children seem to have been born together. Many of the rhymes are nonsense jingles; boys and girls all over the world have used them for bouncing balls, skipping rope, and counting:*

*"Eenie, meenie, minie, mo..."*

*"Onery, twoery, tickery, tin..."*

*"Ibbity, bibbity, sibbity, sab..."*

*But the best of the little poems are about people. Scattered through the following pages are rhymes about people who really lived...such as Charlie, who was Prince Charles of England; Georgie Porgie, the pudgy boy who grew up to be King George; jolly old King Cole— all are part of Mother Goose's large, wonderful family.*

## Jack Horner

Little Jack Horner
Sat in a corner,
   Eating a Christmas pie.
He put in his thumb
And pulled out a plum,
   And said, "What a good boy am I!"

## Curlylocks

Curlylocks! Curlylocks!
   Wilt thou be mine?
Thou shalt not wash dishes
   Nor yet feed the swine;
But sit on a cushion
   And sew a fine seam,
And feast upon strawberries,
   Sugar and cream.

## One Girl

Elizabeth, Elspeth, Betsy, and Bess,
They all went together to seek a bird's nest.
They found a bird's nest with five eggs in,
They all took one, and left four in.

122

## Baby Bunting

Bye, baby bunting,
Daddy's gone a-hunting,
To get a little rabbit-skin
To wrap his baby bunting in.

## The Man in the Moon

The man in the moon
Came down too soon
To inquire his way to Norwich.
He went to the south
And burnt his mouth
While eating hot pease porridge.

## A Crooked Man

There was a crooked man, and he went a crooked mile.
He found a crooked sixpence against a crooked stile:
He bought a crooked cat, which caught a crooked mouse,
And they all lived together in a little crooked house.

123

## Barber

"Barber, barber, shave a pig;
How many hairs will make a wig?"
"Four and twenty, that's enough."
Give the barber a pinch of snuff.

## Old King Cole

Old King Cole
Was a merry old soul,
    And a merry old soul was he;
He called for his pipe,
And he called for his bowl,
    And he called for his fiddlers three.

Every fiddler
He had a fiddle,
    And a very fine fiddle had he.
"Tweedle-tweedle-dee" went the fiddlers
"Tweedle-tweedle-deedle-deedle-dee."

Oh, there's none so rare
As can compare
    With King Cole and his fiddlers three!

## Georgie Porgie

Georgie Porgie, pudding and pie,
Kissed the girls and made them cry;
When the girls came out to play,
Georgie Porgie ran away.

## Tom Tucker

Little Tom Tucker
Sings for his supper;
What shall he eat?
White bread and butter.
How shall he cut it,
Without e'er a knife?
How will he be married
Without e'er a wife?

## Charley

Over the water, and over the sea,
And over the water to Charley;
Charley loves good ale and wine,
And Charley loves good brandy,
And Charley loves a pretty girl,
As sweet as sugar-candy.

Over the water and over the sea,
And over the water to Charley;
I'll have none of your nasty beef,
Nor I'll have none of your barley;
But I'll have some of your very best flour,
To make a white cake for my Charley.

## Doctor Foster

Doctor Foster went to Glo'ster
In a shower of rain;
He stepped in a puddle, up to his middle,
And never went there again.

## Mary

"Mary, Mary, quite contrary,
  How does your garden grow?"
"With cockle-shells and silver bells
  And pretty maids all in a row."

## Recipe for Children

What are little boys made of, made of?
What are little boys made of?
Snips and snails, and puppy dogs' tails,
And that's what little boys are made of, made of.

What are little girls made of, made of?
What are little girls made of?
Sugar and spice, and everything nice,
And that's what little girls are made of, made of.

## A Fine Lady

Ride a cock-horse
　　to Banbury Cross
To see a fine lady
　　upon a white horse.
Rings on her fingers
　　and bells on her toes,
She shall have music
　　wherever she goes.

## Little Boy Blue

Little Boy Blue, come blow your horn,
The sheep's in the meadow, the cow's in the corn;
But where is the boy that looks after the sheep?
He's under the hay-cock, fast asleep.
Will you awake him? No, not I;
For if I do, he'll be sure to cry.

## A Song of Sixpence

Sing a song of sixpence,
   A pocket full of rye;
Four and twenty blackbirds
   Baked in a pie;

When the pie was opened,
   The birds began to sing;
Was not that a dainty dish
   To set before the king?

The king was in his counting-house
   Counting out his money;
The queen was in the parlor
   Eating bread and honey;

The maid was in the garden
   Hanging out the clothes,
When along came a blackbird
   And pecked off her nose.

## Jack Spratt

Jack Spratt
  could eat no fat,
His wife could eat
  no lean;
And so, betwixt them both
  you see,
They licked
  the platter clean.

## Girls and Boys

Girls and boys, come out to play;
The moon doth shine as bright as day;

Leave your supper, and leave your sleep,
And come with your playfellows into the street.

Come with a whoop, come with a call,
Come with a good will or not at all.

Up the ladder and down the wall,
A halfpenny roll will serve us all.

You find milk, and I'll find flour,
And we'll have a pudding in half-an-hour.

## Three Wise Men

Three wise men of Gotham
Went to sea in a bowl.
If the bowl had been stronger
My song had been longer.

## A Little Husband

I had a little husband
   No bigger than my thumb;
I put him in a pint pot,
   And there I bade him drum.

I bought a little horse,
   That galloped up and down;
I bridled him and saddled him,
   And sent him out of town.

I gave him some garters,
   To garter up his hose,
And a little pocket handkerchief,
   To wipe his pretty nose.

## Little Bo-Peep

Little Bo-peep has lost her sheep,
   And can't tell where to find them;
Leave them alone, and they'll come home,
   And bring their tails behind them.

Little Bo-peep fell fast asleep,
   And dreamed she heard them bleating;
But when she awoke, she found it a joke,
   For they were still a-fleeting.

131

## Wee Willy Winkie

*Wee Willy Winkie runs through the town,*
*Upstairs and downstairs in his nightgown,*
*Tapping at the window, peeping at the lock:—*
*"Are all the babes gone to bed? It's now ten o'clock!"*

132

## Miss Muffet

Little Miss Muffet,
Sat on a tuffet,
Eating her curds and whey;
There came a great spider
That sat down beside her,
And frightened Miss Muffet away.

## Peter

Peter, Peter, pumpkin eater,
Had a wife and couldn't keep her.
He put her in a pumpkin shell,
And there he kept her very well.

## Taffy

Taffy was a Welshman, Taffy was a thief;
Taffy came to my house and stole a piece of beef.

I went to Taffy's house, Taffy was not home;
Taffy came to my house and stole a marrow-bone.

I went to Taffy's house, Taffy was in bed;
I took the marrow-bone and beat him on the head.

## Man in Leather

One misty, moisty morning,
    When cloudy was the weather,
I met a little old man
    Clothed all in leather.

He began to bow and scrape,
    And I began to grin—
"How do you do, and how do you do,
    And how do you do again!"

## Three Men

Rub-a-dub-dub,
Three men in a tub,
And who do you think they be?
The butcher, the baker,
The candlestick-maker;
Turn 'em out, knaves all three!

## Peter Piper

Peter Piper picked a peck of pickled peppers;
A peck of pickled peppers Peter Piper picked;
If Peter Piper picked a peck of pickled peppers,
Where's the peck of pickled peppers Peter Piper picked?

*"The King of the Cats"*
*has had a long history.*
*It is an old wives' tale in England,*
*but older versions have been found in France and Scandinavia.*
*In our own time Stephen Vincent Benét made it into*
*a comedy with a touch of terror.*
*The following version, which is the most recent,*
*turns the tale back into pure fantasy.*

# The King of the Cats

### RETOLD BY MICHAEL LEWIS

IN A quiet part of the country there lived a farmer and his wife and their cat, a large silver-gray Maltese who was called Mister. They had been together for many years, far away from the noise of the city and, though they were sometimes lonely, nothing ever happened to disturb their peace and happiness.

One night, however, the farmer came home in a state of great agitation. "What is it?" asked his wife. "I've never seen you so disturbed."

"Reason enough," he replied. "I've got to find Master Morton."

"Who may Master Morton be?" asked his wife. "And why must you find him?"

"I'll tell you if you'll stop asking questions. You'll find it hard to believe. Just the same, the truth is I was walking down the lane that skirts the woods—I was later than usual and it had grown dark. Keeping my eyes on the path, I suddenly saw a queer sight ahead of me. It was—and at first I thought I must be out of my mind—a small procession. It was a procession of cats! What made it queerer was that the procession was led by six black cats who were carrying something. With a shudder I realized they were carrying a coffin. And they all cried—yes, they really *cried*—a kind of mournful 'miaow.'"

The farmer's cat, who was sitting near the hearth, looked up and echoed the sound.

"Miaow," he cried.

"Then, when I looked closer, I saw that the coffin was covered with a piece of purple velvet and—of all things—it was embroidered in gold! There was just light enough for me to make out a pattern of gold crowns. The cats did not seem to mind my watching them. In fact, they looked as if they wanted to say

135

something; but all I could make out was that unhappy 'miaow.'"

"Miaow, miaow," once more echoed the farmer's cat.

"Suddenly the funeral procession stopped, and the leader lifted up his head and spoke to me. He spoke, mind you, in English! What he said was this: 'Tell Master Morton that Merton is dead'— whatever that means."

"Look! Look at Mister!" cried his wife. "He seems possessed!"

The farmer looked—and the cat on the hearth swelled up to twice his usual size. His eyes blazed and his tail stood up straight as a scepter. Then he screamed: "I'm Master Morton—and if Merton is dead, then I am King of the Cats!"

With sparks flying from his fur, he bolted through the door and vanished into the night. A moment later there was a great chorus outside—"Miaow! Miaow! Miaow!"—it sounded like rejoicing. Then all was still and lonely again.

# The Elves and the Shoemaker

## BY JAKOB AND WILHELM GRIMM

THERE WAS once a shoemaker who, through no fault of his own, became so poor that at last he had nothing left but just enough leather to make one pair of shoes. He cut out the shoes at night, so as to set to work upon them next morning; and as he had a good conscience, he laid himself quietly down in his bed, committed himself to heaven, and fell asleep.

In the morning, after he had said his prayers and was going to get to work, he found the pair of shoes made and finished, and standing on his table. He was very much astonished, and could not tell what to think. He took the shoes in his hand to examine them. They were so well made that every stitch was in its right place, just as if they had come from the hand of a master workman.

138

Soon after, a purchaser entered, and as the shoes fitted him very well, he gave more than the usual price for them. The shoemaker now had enough money to buy leather for two more pairs of shoes. He cut them out at night, and intended to set to work the next morning with fresh spirit. But that was not to be, for when he got up the shoes were already finished. Even a customer was not lacking, who gave him so much money that he was able to buy leather enough for four new pairs.

Early next morning the shoemaker found the four pairs also finished, and so it always happened; whatever he cut out in the evening was worked up by the morning, so that he was soon in the way of making a good living, and in the end became very well-to-do.

One night not long before Christmas, when the shoemaker had finished cutting out, and before he went to bed, he said to his wife, "How would it be if we were to sit up tonight and see who it is that does us this service?"

His wife agreed, and set a light to burn. Then they both hid in a corner of the room behind some coats that were hanging up, and they began to watch.

As soon as it was midnight they saw come in two neatly formed naked little men, who seated themselves before the shoemaker's table and took up the work that was already prepared. They began to stitch, to pierce, and to hammer so cleverly and quickly with their little fingers that the shoemaker's eyes could scarcely follow them, so full of wonder was he. And they never left off until everything was finished and was standing ready on the table, and then they jumped up and ran off.

The next morning the shoemaker's wife said to her husband, "Those little men have made us rich, and we ought to show ourselves grateful. With all their running about, and having nothing to cover them, they must be very cold. I'll tell you what: I will make little shirts, coats, waistcoats, and breeches for them, and knit each of them a pair of stockings, and you shall make each of them a pair of shoes."

The husband consented willingly, and at night, when everything was finished, they laid the gifts together on the table, instead of the cut-out work, and placed themselves so that they could observe how the little men would behave.

When midnight came, the two little men rushed in, ready to set to work. When they found the neat little garments put ready for them, instead of the pieces of prepared leather, they stood a moment in surprise. Then they showed the greatest delight. With the greatest swiftness they took up the pretty garments and slipped them on, singing,

"What spruce and dandy
     boys are we!
No longer cobblers
     we will be."

Then they hopped and danced about, jumping over the chairs and tables, and at last they danced out the door.

From that time they were never seen again; but it always went well with the shoemaker as long as he lived, and whatever he took in hand prospered.

# The Five Marvelous Pretzels

### BY CARL SANDBURG

FIVE NIGHTS before Christmas, five pretzels sit looking out of a grocery window lighted by five candles. And outside they see snow falling, big white snowflakes coming down cool and quiet. And they see a man come along and stop in front of the window and he looks in while they look out. They see his right hand brush off snow from his left shoulder and his left hand brush off snow from his right shoulder. And they see him shake off snow from his hat and put his hat back on his head. But they don't hear the man saying, "Well, well, here are five pretzels. And how many children is it I have at home running around upstairs and downstairs, in and out of corners? One, two, three, four, five, one for each pretzel."

Now early that afternoon they decide

they will go with a circus and be trapeze actors. On billboards everywhere people will see in big letters

THE FIVE
MARVELOUS PRETZELS!

And just before they run out of their dressing rooms in pink tights and bow to the audience and throw kisses to the audience, one kiss with the right hand and the other kiss with the left hand, a man with a big musical megaphone calls to the audience

"THE FIVE
MARVELOUS PRETZELS!"

Then up in the air they go and two of them hang by their knees and throw the other three pretzels back and forth in the air, in the empty and circumambient air.

So far, so good.

Then comes the argument, the fuss, the dispute. Which two shall hang by their knees and which three shall be thrown back and forth in the empty and circumambient air? All five want to be the two that hang by their knees. None of them wants to be one of the three thrown back and forth. So they say, "Let's forget it."

Now they decide instead they will ride on the heads of the first five elephants in the vast mammoth stupendous parade of the elephants. On billboards people will see five elephants and on the head of each mammoth stupendous elephant rides one dazzling glittering little pretzel, in pink tights, bowing and throwing kisses to the audience, one kiss with the right hand and the other kiss with the left hand. Yes, so they decide. And they will have it fixed that just before the first elephant comes out leading the parade a man with a big musical megaphone calls to the audience

### "THE FIVE MARVELOUS PRETZELS!"

So far, so good.

Then comes the argument. Who should ride on the head of the first elephant? Who should be the first one to come out bowing and throwing kisses to the audience? They argue, they fuss, they dispute, they wrangle. And at last they decide that whoever rides the first elephant today rides the last elephant tomorrow.

Then they see the man who stands looking in where they are looking out, brushing snow off his right shoulder with his left hand, brushing snow off his left shoulder with his right hand, shaking snow off his hat and putting it back on his head.

And the man walks into the store, pays ten cents and comes out with the five pretzels in a paper sack and walks along the street in the falling snow, big white snowflakes coming down cool and quiet on his shoulders, on his hat.

And does he know as he walks along in the falling snow what happens that afternoon and evening?

No.

Does he know he has in a paper sack

### THE FIVE MARVELOUS PRETZELS!

No.

Does he know they decide to go with a circus and be trapeze actors and then change their minds?

No.

Does he know they decide instead they will ride on the heads of five elphants and bow and throw kisses to the audience while thousands of people laugh and cheer and cry, "Look, look, look, here come the five marvelous pretzels"?

No.

Then what does the man know about what the five pretzels want to be? Nothing, absolutely nothing.

Which shows *how* ignorant some people are!

# The Traveling Musicians

### BY JAKOB AND WILHELM GRIMM

AN HONEST farmer had once an ass that had been a faithful servant to him a great many years, but was now growing old and every day more and more unfit for work. His master therefore was tired of keeping him and began to think of putting an end to him; but the ass, who saw that some mischief was in the wind, took himself slyly off, and began his journey towards Bremen, "for there," thought he, "I may chance to be chosen town musician."

After he had traveled a little way, he spied a dog lying by the roadside and panting as if he were tired. "What makes you pant so, my friend?" said the ass. "Alas!" said the dog, "my master was going to knock me on the head, because I am old and weak, and can no longer make myself useful to him in hunting; so I ran away; but what can I do to earn my livelihood?" "Hark ye!" said the ass, "I am going to Bremen to turn musician: suppose you go with me, and try what you can do in the same way?" The dog said he was willing, and they jogged on together.

They had not gone far before they saw a cat sitting in the middle of the road and making a most rueful face. "Pray my good lady," said the ass, "what's the matter with you? You look quite out of spirits!" "Ah me!" said the cat, "How can one be in good spirits when one's life is in danger? Because I am beginning to grow old and had rather lie at my ease by the fire than run about the house after the mice, my mistress laid hold of me, and was going to drown me; and though I have been lucky enough to get away from her, I do not know what I am to live upon." "Oh!" said the ass, "by all means go with us to Bremen; you are a good night singer, and may make your fortune." The cat was pleased with the thought, and joined the party.

Soon afterwards, as they were passing by a farmyard, they saw a cock perched upon a gate, and screaming out with all his might and main. "Bravo!" said the ass; "upon my word you make a famous noise; pray what is all this about?"

"Why," said the cock, "I was just now saying that we should have fine weather for our washing-day, and yet my mistress and the cook don't thank me for my pains, but threaten to cut off my head tomorrow, and make broth of me for the guests that are coming on Sunday!" "Heaven forbid!" said the ass; "come with us, Master Chanticleer; it will be better, at any rate, than staying here to have your head cut off! Besides, who knows? If we take care to sing in tune, we may get up some kind of a concert: so come along with us." "With all my heart," said the cock; so they all four went on jollily together.

They could not, however, reach the town the first day; so when night came on, they went into a wood to sleep. The ass and the dog laid themselves down under a great tree, and the cat climbed into the branches; while the cock, thinking that the higher he sat the safer he should be, flew up to the very top of the tree, and then, according to his custom, before he went to sleep, looked out on all sides of him to see that everything was well. In doing this, he saw afar off something bright and shining; and calling to his companions said, "There must be a house no great way off, for I see a light." "If that be the case," said the ass, "we had better change our quarters, for our lodging is not the best in the world!" "Besides," added the dog, "I should not be the worse for a bone or two, or a bit of meat." So they walked off together towards the spot where Chanticleer had seen the light; and as they drew near, it became larger and brighter, till they at last came close to a house in which a gang of robbers lived.

The ass, being the tallest of the company, marched up to the window and peeped in. "Well, Donkey," said Chanticleer, "what do you see?" "What do I see?" replied the ass; "why, I see a table spread with all kinds of good things, and robbers sitting round it making merry." "That would be a noble lodging for us," said the cock. "Yes," said the ass, "if we could only get in"; so they consulted together how they should contrive to get the robbers out; and at last they hit upon a plan. The ass placed himself upright on his hind-legs, with his fore-feet resting against the window; the dog got upon his back; the cat scrambled up to the dog's shoulders, and the cock flew up and sat upon the cat's head. When all

was ready, a signal was given, and they began their music. The ass brayed, the dog barked, the cat mewed, and the cock screamed; and then they all broke through the window at once and came tumbling into the room, amongst the broken glass, with a most hideous clatter! The robbers, who had been not a little frightened by the opening concert, had now no doubt that some frightful hobgoblin had broken in upon them, and scampered away as fast as they could.

The coast once clear, our travellers soon sat down, and dispatched what the robbers had left, with as much eagerness as if they had not expected to eat again for a month. As soon as they had satisfied themselves, they put out the lights, and each once more sought out a resting-place to his own liking. The donkey laid himself down upon a heap of straw in the yard; the dog stretched himself upon a mat behind the door; the cat rolled herself up on the hearth before the warm ashes; and the cock perched upon a beam on the top of the house; and as they were all rather tired with their journey, they soon fell asleep.

But about midnight, when the robbers saw from afar that the lights were out and that all seemed quiet, they began to think that they had been in too great a hurry to run away; and one of them, who was bolder than the rest, went to see what was going on. Finding everything still, he marched into the kitchen, and groped about till he found a match in order to light a candle; and then, espying the glittering fiery eyes of the cat, he mistook them for live coals, and held the match to them to light it. But the cat, not understanding this joke, sprang at his face, and spat, and scratched at him. This frightened him dreadfully, and away he ran to the back-door; but there the dog jumped up and bit him in the leg; and as he was crossing over the yard the ass kicked him; and the cock, who had been awakened by the noise, crowed with all his might. At this the robber ran back as fast as he could to his comrades, and told the captain "how a horrid witch had got into the house, and had spat at him and scratched his face with her long bony fingers; how a man with a knife in his hand had hidden himself behind the door, and stabbed him in the leg; how a black monster stood in the yard and struck him with a club; and how the devil sat upon the top of the house, and cried out, 'Throw the rascal up here!'" After this the robbers never dared to go back to the house; but the musicians were so pleased with their quarters that they took up their abode there; and there they are, I dare say, at this very day.

*His name was Blunder—and he was well named.*
*He got into trouble because he did not really*
*hear what was said to him,*
*because he did not really see what he was looking at,*
*and because he was apt to forget the very thing*
*for which he was supposed to be looking.*

# Blunder

## BY LOUISE E. CHOLLET

BLUNDER was going to the Wishing-Gate, to wish for a pair of Shetland ponies, and a little coach, like Tom Thumb's. And of course you can have your wish, if you once get there. But the thing is, to find it; for it is not, as you imagine, a great gate, with a tall marble pillar on each side, and a sign over the top, like this, WISHING GATE—but just an old stile, made of three sticks. Put up two fingers, cross them on the top with another finger, and you have it exactly,—the way it looks, I mean,—a worm-eaten stile, in a meadow; and as there are plenty of old stiles in meadows, how are you to know which is the one?

Blunder's fairy godmother knew, but then she could not tell him, for that was not according to fairy rules and regulations. She could only direct him to follow the road, and ask the way of the first owl he met; and over and over she charged him, for Blunder was a very careless little boy, and seldom found anything, "Be sure you don't miss him,—be sure you don't pass him by." And so far Blunder had come on very well, for the road was straight; but at the turn it forked. Should he go through the wood, or turn to the right? There was an owl nodding in a tall oak-tree, the first owl Blunder had seen; but he was a little afraid to wake him up, for Blunder's fairy godmother had told him that this was a great philosopher, who sat up all night to study the habits of frogs and mice, and knew everything but what went on in the daylight, under his nose; and he could think of nothing better to say to this great philosopher than "Good Mr. Owl, will you please show me the way to the Wishing-Gate?"

"Eh! what's that?" cried the owl, starting out of his nap. "Have you brought me a frog?"

"No," said Blunder, "I did not know that you would like one. Can you tell me the way to the Wishing-Gate?"

"Wishing-Gate! Wishing-Gate!" hooted the owl, very angry. "Winks and naps! how dare you disturb me for such a thing as that? Do you take me for a mile-stone! Follow your nose, sir, follow your nose!" —and, ruffling up his feathers, the owl was asleep again in a moment.

But how could Blunder follow his nose? His nose would turn to the right, or take him through the woods, whichever way his legs went, and "what was the use of asking the owl," thought Blunder, "if this was all?" While he hesitated, a chipmunk came scurrying down the path, and, seeing Blunder, stopped short with a little squeak.

"Good Mrs. Chipmunk," said Blunder, "can you tell me the way to the Wishing-Gate?"

"I can't, indeed," answered the chipmunk, politely. "What with getting in nuts, and the care of a young family, I have so little time to visit anything! But if you will follow the brook, you will find an old water-sprite under a slanting stone, over which the water pours all day with a noise like wabble! wabble! who, I have no doubt, can tell you all about it. You will know him, for he does nothing but grumble about the good old times when a brook would have dried up before it would have turned a mill-wheel."

So Blunder went on up the brook, and, seeing nothing of the water-sprite, or the slanting stone, was just saying to himself, "I am sure I don't know where he is,—I can't find it," when he spied a frog sitting on a wet stone.

"Mr. Frog," asked Blunder, "can you tell me the way to the Wishing-Gate?"

"I cannot," said the frog. "I am very sorry, but the fact is I am an artist. Young as I am, my voice is already remarked at our concerts, and I devote myself so entirely to my profession of music, that I have not time to acquire general information. But in a pine-tree beyond, you will find an old crow, who, I am quite sure, can show you the way, as he is a traveller, and a bird of an inquiring turn of mind."

"I don't know where the pine is,—I am sure I can never find him," answered Blunder, discontentedly; but still he went on up the brook, till, hot and tired, and out of patience at seeing neither crow nor pine, he sat down under a great tree to rest. There he heard tiny voices squabbling.

"Get out! Go away, I tell you! It has been knock! knock! knock! at my door all day, till I am tired out. First a wasp, and then a bee, and then another wasp, and then another bee, and now *you*. Go away! I won't let another one in to-day."

"But I want my honey."
"And I want my nap."
"I will come in."
"You shall not."
"You are a miserly old elf."
"And you are a brute of a bee."

And looking about him, Blunder spied a bee, quarrelling with a morning-glory elf, who was shutting up the morning-glory in his face.

"Elf, do you know which is the way to the Wishing-Gate?" asked Blunder.

"No," said the elf, "I don't know anything about geography. I was always too delicate to study. But if you will keep on in this path, you will meet the Dreamman, coming down from fairyland, with his bags of dreams on his shoulder; and if anybody can tell you about the Wishing-Gate, he can."

"But how can I find him?" asked Blunder, more and more impatiently.

"I don't know, I am sure," answered the elf, "unless you should look for him."

So there was no help for it but to go on; and presently Blunder passed the Dreamman, asleep under a witch-hazel, with his bags of good and bad dreams laid over him to keep him from fluttering away. But Blunder had a habit of not using his eyes; for at home, when told to find anything, he always said, "I don't know where it is," or, "I can't find it," and then his mother or sister went straight and found it for him. So he passed the Dreamman without seeing him, and went on till he stumbled on Jack-o'-Lantern.

"Can you show me the way to the Wishing-Gate?" said Blunder.

"Certainly, with pleasure," answered Jack, and, catching up his lantern, set out at once.

Blunder followed close, but, in watching the lantern, he forgot to look to his feet, and fell into a hole filled with black mud.

"I say! the Wishing-Gate is not down there," called out Jack, whisking off among the tree-tops.

"But I can't come up there," whimpered Blunder.

"That is not my fault, then," answered Jack, merrily, dancing out of sight.

O, a very angry little boy was Blunder, when he clambered out of the hole. "I don't know where it is," he said, crying; "I can't find it, and I'll go straight home."

Just then he stepped on an old, moss-grown, rotten stump; and it happened, unluckily, that this rotten stump was a wood-goblin's chimney, Blunder fell through, headlong, in among the pots and pans, in which the goblin's cook was cooking the goblin's supper. The old goblin, who was asleep upstairs, started up in a fright at the tremendous clash and clatter, and, finding that his house was not tumbling about his ears, as he thought at first, stumped down to the kitchen to see what was the matter. The cook heard him coming, and looked about her in a fright to hide Blunder.

"Quick!" cried she. "If my master catches you, he will have you in a pie. In the next room stands a pair of shoes. Jump into them, and they will take you up the chimney."

Off flew Blunder, burst open the door, and tore frantically about the room, in one corner of which stood the shoes; but of course he could not see them, because he was not in the habit of using his eyes.

"I can't find them! O, I can't find them!" sobbed poor little Blunder, running back to the cook.

"Run into the closet," said the cook.

Blunder made a dash at the window, but—"I don't know where it is," he called out.

Clump! clump! That was the goblin half-way down the stairs.

"Goodness gracious mercy me!" exclaimed the cook. "He is coming. The boy

will be eaten in spite of me. Jump into the meal-chest."

"I don't see it," squeaked Blunder, rushing towards the fireplace. "Where is it?"

Clump! clump! That was the goblin at the foot of the stairs, and coming towards the kitchen door.

"There is an invisible cloak hanging on that peg. Get into that," cried the cook, quite beside herself.

But Blunder could no more see the cloak than he could see the shoes, the closet, and the meal-chest; and no doubt the goblin, whose hand was on the latch, would have found him prancing around the kitchen, and crying out, "I can't find

152

it," but, fortunately for himself, Blunder caught his foot in the invisible cloak, and tumbled down, pulling the cloak over him. There he lay, hardly daring to breathe.

"What was all that noise about?" asked the goblin, coming into the kitchen.

"Only my pans, master," answered the cook; and as he could see nothing amiss, the old goblin went grumbling upstairs again, while the shoes the cook gave him took Blunder up the chimney, and landed him in a meadow, safe enough, but so miserable! He was cross, he was disappointed, he was hungry. It was dark, he did not know the way home, and, seeing

an old stile, he climbed up, and sat down on the top of it, for he was too tired to stir. Just then came along the South Wind, with his pockets crammed full of showers, and, as he happened to be going Blunder's way, he took Blunder home; at which the boy was glad enough, only he would have liked it better if the Wind would not have laughed all the way. For what would you think, if you were walking along a road with a fat old gentleman, who went chuckling to himself, and slapping his knees, and poking himself, till he was purple in the face, when he would burst out in a great windy roar of laughter every other minute?

"What *are* you laughing at?" asked Blunder, at last.

"At two things that I saw in my travels," answered the Wind;—"a hen, that died of starvation, sitting on an empty peck-measure that stood in front of a bushel of grain; and a little boy who sat on the top of the Wishing-Gate, and came home because he could not find it."

"What? what's that?" cried Blunder; but just then he found himself at home. There sat his fairy godmother by the fire, her mouse-skin cloak hung up on a peg, and toeing off a spider's-silk stocking an eighth of an inch long; and though everybody else cried, "What luck?" and, "Where is the Wishing-Gate?" she sat mum.

"I don't know where it is," answered Blunder. "I couldn't find it;"—and thereon told the story of his troubles.

"Poor boy!" said his mother, kissing him, while his sister ran to bring him some bread and milk.

"Yes, that is all very fine," cried his godmother, pulling out her needles, and rolling up her ball of silk; "but now hear my story. There was once a little boy who must needs go to the Wishing-Gate, and his fairy godmother showed him the road as far as the turn, and told him to ask the first owl he met what to do then; but this little boy seldom used his eyes, so he passed the first owl, and waked up the wrong owl; so he passed the water-sprite, and found only a frog; so he sat down under the pine-tree, and never saw the crow; so he passed the Dream-man, and ran after Jack-o'-Lantern; so he tumbled down the goblin's chimney, and couldn't find the shoes and the closet and the chest and the cloak; and so he sat on the top of the Wishing-Gate till the South Wind brought him home, and never knew it. Ugh! Bah!" And away went the fairy godmother up the chimney, in such deep disgust that she did not even stop for her mouse-skin cloak.

# Selected Verse

## BY CHRISTINA ROSSETTI

### A Lesson

Hurt no living thing:
   Ladybird, nor butterfly,
Nor moth with dusty wing,
   Nor cricket chirping cheerily,
Nor grasshopper so light of leap,
   Nor dancing gnat, nor beetle fat,
Nor harmless worms that creep.
   Hurt no living thing.

### The Caterpillar

Brown and furry
Caterpillar in a hurry,
Take your walk
To the shady leaf, or stalk,
Or what not,
Which may be the chosen spot.
No toad spy you,
Hovering bird of prey pass by you;
Spin and die,
To live again a butterfly.

### Little Lamb

A motherless soft lambkin
   Alone upon a hill;
No mother's fleece to shelter him
   And wrap him from the cold.
I'll run to him and comfort him,
   I'll fetch him, that I will;
I'll care for him and feed him
   Until he's strong and bold.

### Who Has Seen the Wind?

Who has seen the wind?
  Neither I nor you:
But when the leaves hang trembling
  The wind is passing through.

Who has seen the wind?
  Neither you nor I:
But when the trees bow down their heads
  The wind is passing by.

### Boats and Bridges

Boats sail on the rivers,
  And ships sail on the seas;
But clouds that sail across the sky
  Are prettier far than these.
There are bridges on the rivers,
  As pretty as you please;
But the bow that bridges heaven,
  And overtops the trees,
And builds a road from earth to sky,
  Is prettier far than these.

156

## THE DOLL

All the bells were ringing
And all the birds were singing,
When Molly sat down crying
  For her broken doll:
O you silly Moll!
Sobbing and sighing
  For a broken doll,
When all the bells are ringing,
And all the birds are singing!

## A TOADSTOOL

A toadstool comes up in a night—
  Learn the lesson, little folk.
An oak grows on a hundred years,
  But then it is an oak.

## IF I WERE A QUEEN

If I were a Queen,
  What would I do?
I'd make you King,
  And I'd wait on you.

If I were a King,
  What would I do?
I'd make you Queen,
  And I'd marry you.

157

## MINNIE, MATTIE, AND MAY

Minnie and Mattie
  And fat little May,
Out in the country,
  Spending a day.

Such a bright day,
  With the sun glowing,
And the trees half in leaf,
  And the grass growing.

Pinky white pigling
  Squeals through his snout,
Woolly white lambkin
  Frisks all about.

Cluck! cluck! the nursing hen
  Summons her folk,
Ducklings all downy soft
  Yellow as yolk.

Cluck! cluck! the mother hen
  Summons her chickens
To peck the dainty bits
  Found in her pickings.

Minnie and Mattie
  And May carry posies,
Half of sweet violets,
  Half of primroses.

Give the sun time enough
  Glowing and glowing,
He'll rouse the roses
  And bring them blowing.

Don't wait for roses
  Losing today,
O Minnie, Mattie,
  And wise little May.

Violets and primroses
  Blossom today
For Minnie and Mattie
  And fat little May.

## LULLABY

Lullaby, oh, lullaby!
Flowers are closed and lambs are sleeping;
Lullaby, oh, lullaby!
Stars are up, the moon is peeping;
Lullaby, oh, lullaby!
While the birds are silence keeping,
(Lullaby, oh lullaby!)
Sleep, my baby, fall a-sleeping,
Lullaby, oh lullaby!

## HORSES

The horses of the sea
Rear a foaming crest,
But the horses of the land
Serve us the best.

The horses of the land
Munch corn and clover,
While the foaming sea horses
Toss and turn over.

## WHEN THE COWS COME HOME

When the cows come home the milk is coming,
Honey's made while the bees are humming;
Duck and drake on the rushy lake,
And the deer live safe in the breezy brake;
And timid, funny, brisk little bunny,
Winks his nose and sits all sunny.

## A POCKET HANDKERCHIEF

A pocket handkerchief to hem—
Oh dear, oh dear, oh dear!
How many stitches it will take
Before it's done, I fear.

Yet set a stitch and then a stitch,
And stitch and stitch away,
Till stitch by stitch the hem is done—
And after work is play!

*When Prince Dolor was a baby, his nurse dropped him
and, as a result, he was unable to walk. His father and mother
died when he was still an infant; his wicked uncle imprisoned
the young Prince at the top of a tower in a distant part
of the country. He and a woman caretaker were kept there
until no one remembered that the boy had ever lived.
One day an old lady appeared and told the Prince that she was
his godmother. She gave him a cloth bundle tied up in knots.
This, she said, was his "traveling cloak."*
*The following story is a chapter from* The Little Lame Prince,
*a children's classic that was written more than 100 years ago.*

# *From* The Little Lame Prince

BY DINAH MULOCK CRAIK

## THE TRAVELING CLOAK

When Prince Dolor had patiently untied all the knots, a remarkable thing happened. The cloak began to undo itself. Slowly unfolding, it laid itself down on the carpet, as flat as if it had been ironed. The split joined with a little sharp crick-crack, and the rim turned up all round till it was breast-high. Meantime the cloak had grown and grown, and become quite large enough for one person to sit in it as comfortably as if in a boat.

The Prince watched it rather anxiously; it was such an extraordinary, not to say a frightening, thing. However, he was no coward, but a thorough boy, who, if he had been like other boys, would doubtless have grown up daring and adventurous—a soldier, a sailor, or the like. As it was, he could only show his courage morally, not physically, by being afraid of nothing, and by doing boldly all that it was in his narrow powers to do. And I am not sure but that in this way he showed more real valor than if he had had six pairs of proper legs.

He said to himself: "What a goose I am! As if my dear godmother would ever have given me anything to hurt me. Here goes!"

So, with one of his active leaps, he sprang right into the middle of the cloak, where he squatted down, wrapping his arms tight round his knees, for they shook a little and his heart beat fast. But there he sat, steady and silent, waiting for what might happen next.

Nothing did happen, and he began to think nothing would, and to feel rather disappointed, when he recollected the words he had been told to repeat—"Abracadabra, dum dum dum!"

He repeated them, laughing all the while, they seemed such nonsense. And then—and then—

Now I don't expect anybody to believe what I am going to relate, though a good many wise people have believed a good many sillier things. And as seeing's believing, and I never saw it, I cannot be expected implicitly to believe it myself, except in a sort of way. And yet there is truth in it—for some people.

The cloak rose, slowly and steadily, at first only a few inches, then gradually higher and higher, till it nearly touched the skylight. Prince Dolor's head actually bumped against the glass, or would have done so had he not crouched down, crying, "Oh, please don't hurt me!" in a most melancholy voice.

Then he suddenly remembered his godmother's express command — "Open the skylight!"

Regaining his courage at once, without a moment's delay he lifted up his head and began searching for the bolt—the cloak meanwhile remaining perfectly still, balanced in the air. But the minute the window was opened, out it sailed—right out into the clear, fresh air, with nothing between it and the cloudless blue.

Prince Dolor had never felt any such delicious sensation before. I can understand it. Cannot you? Did you never think, in watching the rooks going home singly or in pairs, soaring their way across the calm evening sky till they vanish like black dots in the misty gray, how pleasant it must feel to be up there, quite out of the noise and din of the world, able to hear and see everything down below, yet troubled by nothing and teased by no one—all alone, but perfectly content?

Something like this was the happiness of the little lame Prince when he got out of Hopeless Tower, and found himself for the first time in the pure open air, with the sky above him and the earth below.

True, there was nothing but earth and sky; no houses, no trees, no rivers, mountains, seas—not a beast on the ground or a bird in the air. But to him even the level plain looked beautiful. And then there was the glorious arch of the sky, with a little young moon sitting in the west like a baby queen. And the evening breeze was so sweet and fresh—it kissed him like his godmother's kisses. And by and by a few stars came out—first two or three, and then quantities—quantities! so that when he began to count them he was utterly bewildered.

By this time, however, the cool breeze had become cold. The mist gathered; and as he had, as he said, no outdoor clothes, poor Prince Dolor was not very comfortable. The dews fell damp on his curls. He began to shiver.

"Perhaps I had better go home," thought he.

But how? For in his excitement the other words which his godmother had told him to use had slipped his memory. They were only a little different from the first, but in that slight difference all the importance lay. As he repeated his "Abracadabra," trying ever so many other syllables after it, the cloak only went faster and faster, skimming on through the dusky, empty air.

The poor little Prince began to feel frightened. What if his wonderful traveling cloak should keep on thus traveling, perhaps to the world's end, carrying with it a poor, tired, hungry boy, who, after all, was beginning to think there was something very pleasant in supper and bed!

"Dear godmother," he cried pitifully, "do help me! Tell me just this once and I'll never forget again."

Instantly the words came rushing into his head—"Abracadabra, tum tum ti!" Was that it? Ah! yes—for the cloak began to turn slowly. He repeated the charm again, more distinctly and firmly, when it gave a gentle dip, like a nod of satisfaction, and immediately started back, as fast as ever, in the direction of the tower.

He reached the skylight, which he found exactly as he had left it, and slipped in, cloak and all, as easily as he had got out. He had scarcely reached the floor, and was still sitting in the middle of his traveling cloak — like a frog on a water-lily leaf, as his godmother had expressed it—when he heard his nurse's voice outside.

"Bless us! what has become of your Royal Highness all this time? To sit stupidly here at the window till it is quite dark, and leave the skylight open, too. Prince! what can you be thinking of? You are the silliest boy I ever knew."

"Am I?" said he absently, and never heeding her crossness; for his only anxiety was lest she might find out what he had been doing.

She would have been a very clever person to have done so. The instant Prince Dolor got off it, the cloak folded itself up into the tiniest possible parcel, tied all its own knots, and rolled itself of its own accord into the farthest and darkest corner of the room. If the nurse had seen it, which she didn't, she would have taken it for a mere bundle of rubbish not worth noticing.

Shutting the skylight with an angry bang, she brought in the supper and lit the candles with her usual unhappy expression of countenance. But Prince Dolor hardly saw it. He saw only, hid in the corner where nobody else would see it, his wonderful traveling cloak. And though his supper was not particularly nice, he ate it heartily, scarcely hearing a word of his nurse's grumbling, which tonight seemed to have taken the place of her sullen silence.

"Poor woman!" he thought, when he paused a minute to listen and look at her with those quiet, happy eyes, so like his mother's. "Poor woman! she hasn't got a traveling cloak!"

And when he was left alone at last, and crept into his little bed, where he lay awake a good while, watching what he called his "sky-garden," all planted with stars, like flowers, his chief thought was—"I must be up very early tomorrow morning, and get my lessons done, and then I'll go traveling all over the world on my beautiful cloak."

So next day he opened his eyes with the sun, and went with a good heart to his lessons. They had hitherto been the chief amusement of his dull life. Now, I am afraid, he found them also a little dull. But he tried to be good—I don't say Prince Dolor always was good, but he generally tried to be—and when his mind went wandering after the dark, dusty corner where lay his precious treasure, he resolutely called it back again.

"For," he said, "how ashamed my godmother would be of me if I grew up a stupid boy!"

But the instant lessons were done, and he was alone in the empty room, he crept across the floor, undid the shabby little bundle, his fingers trembling with eagerness, climbed on the chair, and thence to the table, so as to unbar the skylight—he forgot nothing now—said his magic charm, and was away out the window, as children say, "in a few minutes less than no time."

Nobody missed him. He was accustomed to sit so quietly always that his nurse, though only in the next room, perceived no difference. And besides, she might have gone in and out a dozen times, and it would have been just the same; she never could have found out his absence.

For what do you think the clever godmother did? She took a quantity of moonshine, or some equally convenient material, and made an image, which she set on the window sill reading, or by the table drawing, where it looked so like

Prince Dolor that any common observer would never have guessed the deception. And even the boy would have been puzzled to know which was the image and which was himself.

And all this while the happy little fellow was away, floating in the air on his magic cloak, and seeing all sorts of wonderful things—or they seemed wonderful to him, who had hitherto seen nothing at all.

First, there were the flowers that grew on the plain, which, whenever the cloak came near enough, he strained his eyes to look at. They were very tiny, but very beautiful—white saxifrage, and yellow lotus, and ground thistles, purple and bright, with many others the names of which I do not know. No more did

Prince Dolor, though he tried to find them out by recalling any pictures he had seen of them. But he was too far off; and though it was pleasant enough to admire them as brilliant patches of color, still he would have liked to examine them all. He was, as a little girl I know once said of a playfellow, "a very examining boy."

"I wonder," he thought, "whether I could see better through a pair of glasses like those my nurse reads with, and takes such care of. How I would take care of them, too, if I only had a pair!"

Immediately he felt something queer and hard fixing itself to the bridge of his nose. It was a pair of the prettiest gold spectacles ever seen. Looking downward, he found that, though ever so high above

164

the ground, he could see every minute blade of grass, every tiny bud and flower —nay, even the insects that walked over them.

"Thank you, thank you!" he cried, in a gush of gratitude—to anybody or everybody, but especially to his dear godmother, who he felt sure had given him this new present. He amused himself with it for ever so long, with his chin pressed on the rim of the cloak, gazing down upon the grass, every square foot of which was a mine of wonders.

Then, just to rest his eyes, he turned them up to the sky—the blue, bright, empty sky, which he had looked at so often and seen nothing.

Now surely there was something. A long, black, wavy line, moving on in the distance, not by chance, as the clouds move apparently, but deliberately, as if it were alive. He might have seen it before—he almost thought he had; but then he could not tell what it was. Looking at it through his spectacles, he discovered that it really was alive; being a long string of birds, flying one after the other, their wings moving steadily and their heads pointed in one direction, as steadily as if each were a little ship, guided invisibly by an unerring helm.

"They must be the passage birds flying seaward!" cried the boy, who had read a little about them, and had a great talent for putting two and two together and finding out all he could. "Oh, how I should like to see them quite close, and to know where they come from and whither they are going! How I wish I knew everything in all the world!"

A silly speech for even an "examining" little boy to make; because, as we grow older, the more we know the more we find out there is to know. And Prince Dolor blushed when he had said it, and hoped nobody had heard him.

Apparently somebody had, however. For the cloak gave a sudden bound forward, and presently he found himself high in the air, in the very middle of that band of aerial travelers, who had no magic cloak to travel on—nothing except their wings. Yet there they were, making their fearless way through the sky.

Prince Dolor looked at them as one after the other they glided past him; and they looked at him—those pretty swallows with their changing necks and bright eyes—as if wondering to meet in mid-air such an extraordinary sort of bird.

"Oh, I wish I were going with you, you lovely creatures! I'm getting so tired of this dull plain, and the dreary and lonely tower. I do so want to see the world! Pretty swallows, dear swallows! tell me what it looks like—the beautiful, wonderful world!"

But the swallows flew past him—steadily, slowly pursuing their course as if inside each little head had been a mariner's compass, to guide him safe over land and sea, direct to the place where he wished to go.

The boy looked after them with envy. For a long time he followed with his eyes the faint, wavy black line as it floated away, sometimes changing its curves a little, but never deviating from its settled course, till it vanished entirely out of sight.

Then he settled himself down in the center of the cloak, feeling quite sad and lonely.

"I think I'll go home," said he, and repeated his "Abracadabra, tum tum ti!" with a rather heavy heart.

# The Sorcerer's Apprentice

### RETOLD BY MICHAEL LEWIS

HE WAS a proud boy. And he had a right to be proud. Other boys had to learn shoemaking or brick-laying or hair-cutting; other boys had to take instruction for years before they could become tailors or tinkers or coopers or carpenters. But Hugo was apprenticed to a magician.

The man with whom Hugo studied and for whom he worked was not only a magician but a master magician, a wizard who knew the Great Book of Magic by heart and could read it backward (which is the way all real books of magic are written), and he was always trying something new. He was no longer interested in preparing strange powders or concocting love potions or brewing a variety of poisons—these were things that he had done with his left hand when he was a youth, and now he was old, the oldest sorcerer in the country.

The secret of mortal life—that was what he was after. But, though he had examined every page in the ancient volumes of White, Gray, and Black Magic, and though he had kept a dozen copper kettles boiling with fiery brews and another dozen cauldrons simmering with weirdly bubbling mixtures, he could not create a human being. He could change midges into mice and mice into monsters, but he could not change mice into men.

The sorcerer was disappointed but he was not disheartened; he felt he was getting nearer and nearer to his goal. His latest accomplishment was making life-less things obey him and do whatever labor he demanded. This filled Hugo with pleasure, the more so since it relieved him of most of his daily chores. He watched with fascination as his master commanded the fire to leap higher, the

167

bellows to blow itself, the ladle to leap into the kettle and start stirring, and the broom to clean the kitchen floor. Hugo listened carefully to every odd syllable, followed every gesture, and memorized everything from the crook of a finger to the lifting of an eyebrow.

One evening when the sorcerer had gone to a neighboring town to get some mysterious ingredient, Hugo determined he would experiment. He would not try anything complicated, yet try he would. He would see if he could do something small but useful, simple but magical. An old broom stood in the corner, propped up beside the fireplace. Hugo stood before it and, imitating his master's voice, made a sweeping circle with his hands and recited:

Hocus pocus,
Malus locus,
Make the sinew
Wake within you;
Rouse yourself from your long deep
Sleep.
Tidy the room.
Broom, broom,
Sweep!

Slowly at first, then, as though it were gathering strength, the broom roused itself and began sweeping. It went into every corner, busied itself in every crack, and when the floor was cleared of every speck of dust, it started over again. And over. And over. For a while Hugo was delighted; it proved he had learned his lesson well. But, amused for a little while, soon he grew bored watching the broom's endless sweeping back and forth. He decided to risk something a little harder, something that would require more concentration and greater effort. Closing his eyes, he placed the palms of his hands on top of his head, and, turning his body three times to the left, he recited:

Hocus pocus,
Malus locus,
Broom, broom,
Leave the room;
King's son and queen's daughter,
Go and fetch water;
Never falter.
Quick as a wink,
Fill the sink
To the brink!

The broom stopped short. Hugo, fearing he had failed, held his breath; in another moment he gave a gasp that was part relief and part wonder, for the broom moved over to the threshold, pushed open the door, and went over to the pump. Hugo stared as the broom picked up a pail, worked the pump-handle, and, filling the pail with water, brought it back and emptied it into the sink.

"Faster! Faster!" cried Hugo, excited by what he had done and feeling it would not be long before he could surpass the sorcerer himself. Faster the broom swept from room to pump and back again; it seemed to fly as the drops of water spilled from the splashing pail. It was only after the sink was overflowing that Hugo knew it was time to end the game.

"Enough!" he said. The broom kept on, as though it had not heard. "Stop!" cried Hugo. Then, as the broom refused to obey, he repeated, "Stop! Stop, I tell you!" But the broom kept on fetching and carrying, spilling, slipping and slopping, until the floor was covered with water.

Alarmed, Hugo grew still more frightened as he realized he did not know the magic words for stopping. He tried to recall scraps of a spell for closing doors, putting out the light, bringing silence into a noisy room. But he could not get any further than "Hocus pocus, malus locus, hist, whist, cease, desist..."

And the broom never stopped. The water was up to Hugo's ankles.

Desperate now, Hugo caught the broom in his hands and tightened his fists about it. But the broom had a will of its own; it would not be stopped; it pulled Hugo along, tossed him about, and, with a wild leap into the air, shook him off. Wet to the skin, Hugo picked himself up and stood in the way of the broom. But, gaining new strength with every step, it plunged past Hugo and continued its mad pouring. Breathing hard and with water up to his knees, Hugo suddenly thought of a way to dispose of the broom. He pushed himself over to the wall, seized an axe, and, as the broom approached the sink for the fiftieth time, struck it, splitting it in two.

He chuckled grimly as the two pieces floated on the pool that filled the kitchen. Then, to his horror, he saw the two pieces straighten themselves, increase in length, and turn into *two brooms*—each one working harder and faster than the other.

Night was beginning to fall as the flood reached Hugo's waist. He was in a panic; he could not swim; if the water continued to rise he would surely drown. Only one thing could save him. Hugo prayed as he had never prayed before. Most of all he prayed for the return of the sorcerer. He threshed about, flailing his arms, sobbing and screaming, and still praying.

The water was up to his neck when he saw a dark figure etched in moonlight standing in the doorway. It was, Hugo's pounding heart told him, the sorcerer. Hugo was too agitated to hear what words his master used, but suddenly the busy brooms turned into two broken sticks and the water rapidly receded. Hugo was saved.

Three days later he apprenticed himself to a shoemaker.

*Everyone knows about the naughty rabbit*
*who disobeyed his mother and*
*got into trouble in Mr. McGregor's cabbage patch.*
*Every word of this adventure is familiar;*
*no one would want to change a single syllable.*
*It can never lose its charm*
*for the youngest reader—or the oldest.*

# The Tale of Peter Rabbit

## BY BEATRIX POTTER

"Now, my dears," said old Mrs. Rabbit one morning, "you may go into the fields or down the lane, but don't go into Mr. McGregor's garden: your Father had an accident there; he was put in a pie by Mrs. McGregor. Now run along, and don't get into mischief; I am going out."

Once upon a time there were four little Rabbits, and their names were—

*Flopsy,*
*Mopsy,*
*Cotton-tail,*
*and Peter.*

They lived with their Mother in a sandbank, underneath the root of a very big fir-tree.

was very naughty, ran straight away to Mr. McGregor's garden, and squeezed under the gate!

First he ate some lettuce and some French beans; and then he ate some radishes; and then, feeling rather sick, he went to look for some parsley.

Then old Mrs. Rabbit took a basket and her umbrella, and went through the wood to the baker's. She bought a loaf of brown bread and five currant buns.

Flopsy, Mopsy, and Cotton-tail, who were good little bunnies, went down the lane to gather blackberries; but Peter, who

But round the end of a cucumber frame, whom should he meet but Mr. McGregor!

Mr. McGregor was on his hands and knees planting out young cabbages, but he jumped up and ran after Peter, waving a rake and calling out, "Stop thief!"

171

Peter was most dreadfully frightened; he rushed all over the garden, for he had forgotten the way back to the gate.

He lost one of his shoes among the cabbages, and the other shoe amongst the potatoes.

After losing them, he ran on four legs and went faster, so that I think he might have got away altogether if he had not unfortunately run into a gooseberry net, and got caught by the large buttons on his jacket. It was a blue jacket with brass buttons, quite new.

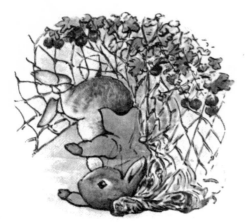

Mr. McGregor was quite sure that Peter was somewhere in the toolshed, perhaps hidden underneath a flower-pot. He began to turn them over carefully, looking under each.

Presently Peter sneezed—"Kertyschoo!" Mr. McGregor was after him in no time, and tried to put his foot upon Peter, who

Peter gave himself up for lost, and shed big tears; but his sobs were overheard by some friendly sparrows, who flew to him in great excitement, and implored him to exert himself.

Mr. McGregor came up with a sieve, which he intended to pop upon the top of Peter; but Peter wriggled out just in time, leaving his jacket behind him. And rushed into the toolshed, and jumped into a can. It would have been a beautiful thing to hide in, if it had not had so much water in it.

After a time he began to wander about, going lippity—lippity—not very fast, and looking all around.

jumped out of the window, upsetting three plants. The window was too small for Mr. McGregor, and he was tired of running after Peter. He went back to his work.

Peter sat down to rest; he was out of breath and trembling with fright, and he had not the least idea which way to go. Also he was very damp with sitting in that can.

He found a door in the wall; but it was locked, and there was no room for a fat little rabbit to squeeze underneath.

An old mouse was running in and out over the stone door-step, carrying peas and beans to her family in the wood. Peter asked her the way to the gate, but she had such a large pea in her mouth that she could not answer. She only shook her head at him. Peter began to cry.

Then he tried to find his way straight across the garden, but he became more and more puzzled. Presently, he came to a pond where Mr. McGregor filled his water-cans. A white cat was staring at some goldfish; she sat very, very still, but now and then the tip of her tail twitched as if it were alive. Peter thought it best to go away without speaking to her; he had heard about cats from his cousin, little Benjamin Bunny.

173

Peter got down very quietly off the wheel-barrow, and started running as fast as he could go, along a straight walk behind some black-currant bushes.

Mr. McGregor caught sight of him at the corner, but Peter did not care. He slipped underneath the gate, and was safe at last in the wood outside the garden.

He went back towards the tool-shed, but suddenly, quite close to him, he heard the noise of a hoe—scr-r-ritch, scratch, scratch, scritch. Peter scuttered underneath the bushes. But presently, as nothing happened, he came out, and climbed upon a wheel-barrow, and peeped over. The first thing he saw was Mr. McGregor hoeing onions. His back was turned towards Peter, and beyond him was the gate!

Mr. McGregor hung up the little jacket and the shoes for a scare-crow to frighten the blackbirds.

Peter never stopped running or looked behind him till he got home to the big fir-tree.

He was so tired that he flopped down upon the nice soft sand on the floor of the rabbit hole, and shut his eyes. His mother was busy cooking; she wondered what he had done with his clothes. It was the second little jacket and pair of shoes that Peter had lost in a fortnight!

I am sorry to say that Peter was not very well during the evening.

His mother put him to bed, and made some camomile tea; and she gave a dose of it to Peter!

"One table-spoonful to be taken at bed-time."

But Flopsy, Mopsy, and Cotton-tail had bread and milk and blackberries for supper.

*"Little Half-Chick" is a folk-tale
that comes from Spain,
where it is called "Medio Pollito."
It is said that in Madrid, the capital city of Spain,
on the top of the highest church stood a weather-vane.
A weather-vane is a metal or wooden figure
which turns with the wind, to show the way the wind is
blowing. This particular weather-vane
showed the outline of a chicken standing on one leg.
The story of "Little Half-Chick" suggests
how it may have got there.*

# Little Half-Chick

### RETOLD BY ANDREW LANG

ONCE upon a time there was a handsome black Spanish hen, who had a large brood of chickens. They were all fine, plump little birds, except the youngest, who was quite unlike his brothers and sisters. Indeed, he was such a strange, queer-looking creature, that when he first chipped his shell his mother could scarcely believe her eyes, he was so different from the twelve other fluffy, downy, soft little chicks who nestled under her wings. This one looked just as if he had been cut in two. He had only one leg, and one wing, and one eye, and he had half a head and half a beak. His mother shook her head sadly as she looked at him and said:

"My youngest born is only a half-chick. He can never grow up a tall handsome cock like his brothers. They will go out into the world and rule over poultry yards of their own; but this poor little fellow will always have to stay at home with his mother."

And she called him Medio Pollito, which is Spanish for half-chick.

176

Now though Medio Pollito was such an odd, helpless-looking little thing, his mother soon found that he was not at all willing to remain under her wing and protection. Indeed, in character he was as unlike his brothers and sisters as he was in appearance. They were good, obedient chickens, and when the old hen chicked after them, they chirped and ran back to her side. But Medio Pollito had a roving spirit in spite of his one leg, and when his mother called to him to return to the coop, he pretended that he could not hear, because he only had one ear.

When she took the whole family out for a walk in the fields, Medio Pollito would hop away by himself, and hide among the Indian corn. Many an anxious minute his brothers and sisters had looking for him, while his mother ran to and fro cackling in fear and dismay.

As he grew older he became more self-willed and disobedient, and his manner to his mother was often very rude, and his temper to the other chickens very disagreeable.

One day he had been out for a longer expedition than usual in the fields. On his return, he strutted up to his mother with the peculiar little hop and kick which was his way of walking, and cocking his one eye at her in a very bold way, he said:

"Mother, I am tired of this life in a dull farmyard, with nothing but a dreary maize field to look at. I'm off to Madrid to see the King."

"To Madrid, Medio Pollito!" exclaimed his mother; "why, you silly chick, it would be a long journey for a grown-up cock, and a poor little thing like you

would be tired out before you had gone half the distance. No, no, stay at home with your mother, and some day, when you are bigger, we will go on a little journey together."

But Medio Pollito had made up his mind, and he would not listen to his mother's advice, nor to the prayers and entreaties of his brothers and sisters.

"What is the use of our all crowding each other up in this poky little place?" he said. "When I have a fine courtyard of my own at the King's palace, I shall perhaps ask some of you to come and pay me a short visit," and scarcely waiting to say good-bye to his family, away he stumped down the high road that led to Madrid.

"Be sure that you are kind and civil to everyone you meet," called his mother, running after him; but he was in such a hurry to be off, that he did not wait to answer her, or even to look back.

A little later in the day, as he was taking a short cut through a field, he passed a stream. Now the stream was all choked up, and overgrown with weeds and water-plants, so that its waters could not flow freely.

"Oh! Medio Pollito," it cried, as the half-chick hopped along its banks, "do come and help me by clearing away these weeds."

"Help you, indeed!" exclaimed Medio Pollito, tossing his head, and shaking the few feathers in his tail. "Do you think I have nothing to do but to waste my time on such trifles? Help yourself, and don't trouble busy travellers. I am off to Madrid to see the King," and hoppity-kick, hoppity-kick, away stumped Medio Pollito.

A little later he came to a fire that had been left by some gipsies in a wood. It was burning very low, and would soon be out.

"Oh! Medio Pollito," cried the fire, in a weak, wavering voice as the half-chick approached, "in a few minutes I shall go quite out, unless you put some sticks and dry leaves upon me. Do help me!"

"Help you, indeed!" answered Medio Pollito. "I have other things to do. Gather sticks for yourself, and don't trouble me. I am off to Madrid to see the King," and hoppity-kick, hoppity-kick, away stumped Medio Pollito.

The next morning, as he was getting near Madrid, he passed a large chestnut tree, in whose branches the wind was caught and entangled. "Oh! Medio Pollito," called the wind, "do hop up here and help me to get free of these branches. I cannot come away, and it is so uncomfortable."

"It is your own fault for going there," answered Medio Pollito. "I can't waste all my morning stopping here to help you. Just shake yourself off, and don't hinder me, for I am off to Madrid to see the King," and hoppity-kick, hoppity-kick, away stumped Medio Pollito in great glee, for the towers and roofs of Madrid were now in sight. When he entered the town he saw before him a great splendid house, with soldiers standing before the gates. This he knew must be the King's palace, and he determined to hop up to the front gate and wait there until the King came out. But as he was hopping past one of the back windows the King's cook saw him:

"Here is the very thing I want," he exclaimed, "for the King has just sent a message to say that he must have chicken broth for his dinner," and, opening the window, he stretched out his arm, caught Medio Pollito, and popped him into the broth-pot that was standing near the fire. Oh! how wet and clammy the water felt

as it went over Medio Pollito's head, making his feathers cling to his side.

"Water, water!" he cried in his despair, "do have pity upon me, and do not wet me like this."

"Ah! Medio Pollito," replied the water, "you would not help me when I was a little stream away on the fields, now you must be punished."

Then the fire began to burn and scald Medio Pollito, and he danced and hopped from one side of the pot to the other, trying to get away from the heat, and crying out in pain:

"Fire, fire! do not scorch me like this; you can't think how it hurts."

"Ah! Medio Pollito," answered the fire, "you would not help me when I was dying away in the wood. You are being punished."

At last, just when the pain was so great that Medio Pollito thought he must die, the cook lifted up the lid of the pot to see if the broth was ready for the King's dinner.

"Look here!" he cried in horror; "this chicken is quite useless. It is burnt to a cinder. I can't send it up to the royal table"; and, opening the window, he threw Medio Pollito out into the street. But the wind caught him up, and whirled him through the air so quickly that Medio Pollito could scarcely breathe, and his heart beat against his side till he thought it would break.

"Oh, wind!" at last he gasped out, "if you hurry me along like this you will kill me. Do let me rest a moment, or—" but he was so breathless that he could not finish the sentence.

"Ah! Medio Pollito," replied the wind, "when I was caught in the branches of the chestnut tree you would not help me; now you are punished." And he swirled Medio Pollito over the roofs of the houses till they reached the highest church in the town, and there he left him fastened to the top of the steeple.

And there stands Medio Pollito this day. And if you go to Madrid and walk through the streets till you come to the highest church, you will see Medio Pollito perched on his one leg on the steeple, with his one wing drooping at his side, and gazing sadly out of his one eye over the town.

# The Prince
## of the Seven Golden Cows

### RETOLD BY BARBARA LEONIE PICARD

A LONG TIME ago there lived in a town in Gascony a prince who had for his coat of arms seven golden cows, and from this he was known as the Prince of the Seven Golden Cows. He was very rich, and of all men in Gascony he was the most generous. Every morning of his life he went to hear Mass, and on leaving the church he would find all the beggars and the poor of the town awaiting him on the church steps, and to each one of them he would give liberally, day after day, so that they would call to heaven to witness his charity and declare, "Prince of the Seven Golden Cows, there is no one like you in all the world. For your sake we would go through fire and water."

Every evening of his life he would feast with his friends: the noblemen and the well-to-do merchants of the town. At his tables were good food and good Gascon wine in abundance, and no guest ever left his castle without a fine gift to carry home; so that they would call to heaven to witness his splendour and his bounty

and declare, "Prince of the Seven Golden Cows, there is no one like you in all the world. For your sake we would go through fire and water."

One day a young man came to the castle and asked to speak with the Prince. He said, "I have heard of your kindness and I am come to beg a favour. There is surely in all this town no one more unfortunate than I. When I was seven years old, my father and my mother died, and since that day I have worked hard to earn my keep. For a few happy months I have been betrothed to a maiden, as good as she was lovely, and we were soon to have married. But this morning she died, and I think that I shall never be happy again. If I knew enough Latin to read the prayers in the prayer book, I would become a monk, but I know no Latin. Have pity on me, Prince of the Seven Golden Cows, and give me fifteen crowns to buy mourning."

"My friend," said the Prince of the Seven Golden Cows, "I am indeed sorry for you. You shall have not fifteen, but one hundred crowns, and may you meet with no more misfortunes."

The young man thanked the Prince of the Seven Golden Cows and went, taking with him the hundred crowns. But after three days he returned, wearing mourning. "Prince of the Seven Golden Cows," he said, "you have been kind to me. There is nothing else for me to live for. Let me be your servant and dwell in your castle, and I will serve you faithfully and ask no wage."

"I would not ask any man's service without paying him his hire," said the Prince. "But if that is as you wish it, it shall be so."

In that manner the young man became a servant in the castle of the Prince of the Seven Golden Cows, and so well he worked and so loyal he showed himself, that the Prince set him over all his other servants. But always the young man wore mourning, so that he came to be known as the Black Steward.

One day he came to the Prince of the Seven Golden Cows. "Lord," he said, "you spend too much on your guests, and you give too much in charity. Within a year your coffers will be empty of gold and silver, and you will be ruined."

"What does that matter?" asked the Prince of the Seven Golden Cows. "I have neither wife nor child to be my heir. I shall spend my gold until it is gone. And when that day comes, I shall still be rich enough, for I have many good friends who will not see me want. Time after time have they told me that for my sake they would go through fire and water."

"You cannot be certain of that," said the Black Steward.

That evening, as they feasted, the Prince of the Seven Golden Cows said to his guests, "Often have you all said to me that you would go through fire and water for my sake, yet today the Black Steward has told me that I cannot be sure of it. How do you answer him, my friends?"

And they one and all cried out against the Black Steward, calling him a rogue. "He steals from you and he cheats you and he cannot be trusted," they said.

The Prince of the Seven Golden Cows sent for the Black Steward. "My friends have called you a thief who steals from his master. Tell me, Black Steward, are they speaking the truth?"

The Black Steward denied nothing. "It is true. I have stolen from you, lord."

In anger the Prince of the Seven Golden Cows drove the Black Steward from his castle, bidding him begone forever. And the Black Steward, who had indeed robbed his master of enough gold to buy a castle, went far from the town to where the River Gers flowed slowly and sleepily past the meadows and vineyards of Gascony; and there, on the bank of the river, he bought a castle and the land around it, and in the castle he waited for what he knew would come to pass.

When a year was all but gone, the Prince of the Seven Golden Cows saw that his coffers were empty and knew that he was ruined. He gave a last banquet for his guests; and when the feasting was over, he said, "My friends, my coffers are all empty and my gold and my silver are spent, and I have nothing left to offer you. So many times have you said to me that for my sake you would go through

182

fire and water. Now that I am ruined, give me your help."

But his guests looked at one another, and their looks were dark, and they scowled. "Prince of the Seven Golden Cows," they said, "you have wasted your wealth in alms-giving. Go, ask the poor for help, not us."

The Prince of the Seven Golden Cows could hardly believe he had heard aright; but when he saw how they turned their backs on him and spoke amongst themselves as though he were not there, he knew that he was not mistaken. He went out to the poor and the beggars, and they called to him for alms. "My friends," he said, "I can give you nothing, for I have nothing left to give. My coffers are all empty and my gold and my silver are spent. But so many times have you told me that for my sake you would go through fire and water that I have no

fears for the future. You are poor, my friends, and you have little, yet will you not share that little with me?"

But the beggars all cried out against him, saying, "You have squandered your wealth in food and wine and in feasting with your guests. Why should we share with you the little we have? Go, beg your bread, even as we do."

The Prince of the Seven Golden Cows could hardly believe he had heard aright; but when he saw how the beggars muttered together, cursing him and shaking their fists because he had nothing to give them, he knew that he was not mistaken.

He stood sadly in his courtyard, crushed between the scorn of his guests and the blame of the poor; and then there came a great clattering of hoofs from the street outside and the baying of many hounds, and into the courtyard rode the Black Steward, a big cudgel in his hands

183

and a pack of huge hounds at his horse's heels.

"After them! Away with them!" cried the Black Steward to the hounds; and they ran, biting and snarling, among the beggars and the noblemen and the well-to-do merchants, whilst the Black Steward himself laid about him with his cudgel, until the courtyard was clear. Then he dismounted and went to where his master stood. "Lord," he said, "they were ungrateful, so I have driven them away."

But the Prince of the Seven Golden Cows looked coldly at the Black Steward. "I ask no services from one who has robbed me," he said.

"Lord, I robbed you that there might be something left to you when you were ruined. On the bank of the River Gers there stands a castle which awaits the arrival of its lord. It is yours."

So the Prince of the Seven Golden Cows left the town forever and went to live in the castle on the quiet bank of the Gers, and there the Black Steward served him without wages, even as he had done in the old days. And so things went on for seven years.

Then, on the last evening of the seventh year, the Prince of the Seven Golden Cows sent for the Black Steward. "In all my life," he said, "I have found but one loyal friend, and that is you. I would tell you my great secret, that you may profit from it when I am gone. Seven years ago, when my coffers were empty and I had spent all my gold and silver on the giving of alms to those who were thankless, and on the feasting of those I believed my friends, I could, had I wished, have gained more riches to replace all I had lost. Yet this I did not do,

because I had at last learnt the ingratitude of all men save myself. But now I am growing old, and within a year I shall be dead. I would wish you, my only friend, to be my heir, so I will tell you the secret of the Seven Golden Cows which are the device of my house. First, fetch an axe, then saddle two horses, and we shall ride forth together."

The Black Steward fetched an axe and saddled two horses, and he and the Prince of the Seven Golden Cows rode out of the castle into the winter's evening. At midnight they reached a cross-roads, close by a marsh where many weeds grew.

"Take your axe," said the Prince of the Seven Golden Cows to the Black Steward, "and cut the tallest of the reeds. But take care, for the reed will seek to protect itself, and it will change its shape three times whilst you are cutting it. Three times only may you strike with your axe, and if by the third stroke you have not cut the reed, you will die in that instant."

The Black Steward took his axe, and going to the tallest of the reeds, he grasped it firmly and raised the axe. At once the reed changed into a serpent with seven hissing heads. But the Black Steward struck boldly, for all the fearsome sight. When he raised his axe for the second stroke, he saw how the reed had become a new-born child. For a moment only he hesitated, then he struck boldly. As he raised his axe for the third stroke, the reed took the likeness of his long-dead betrothed, and the Black Steward trembled and the axe almost dropped from his hand. But he remembered the warning of the Prince of the Seven Golden Cows, and he summoned up all his strength and his courage, and he struck boldly for the last time. And in his left hand he held the tallest of the reeds, severed at the root. He returned to his master.

"You have done well," said the Prince of the Seven Golden Cows. "Now cut from the reed enough to make a flute." When this was done, they returned to the castle.

For the next five months, every night, when the servants of the castle slept, the Prince of the Seven Golden Cows taught the Black Steward a certain tune to play on the flute. And when mid-June was come, and the eve of St. John, the Prince said, "At midnight, bring two cauldrons, six leathern sacks, and the flute, and come with me to the meadow by the river."

At midnight, with the flute, the cauldrons, and the sacks, they stood on the bank of the Gers. "Now play on the flute the tune which I taught you," said the Prince of the Seven Golden Cows.

The Black Steward did as he was bidden, and at once the ground opened, and out of the earth came seven golden cows. They bowed their heads before the Prince and waited. "Milk the cows into the cauldrons," he ordered. So the Black Steward milked the cows into the cauldrons until the cauldrons were full; and the milk of the seven golden cows was golden coins.

"Now fill the sacks with the gold," said the Prince. When it was done, the Prince of the Seven Golden Cows showed the Black Steward a certain spot in the river. "Throw the sacks into the water," he said. As the last sack sank under the water, it was dawn, and the earth opened and the golden cows disappeared.

A month later, the Prince of the Seven Golden Cows was dead, even as he had said. The Black Steward saw him buried with all the splendour fitting to his rank, and then he went to the castle in the town where the Prince had spent his wealth in feasting his guests and in giving alms, and from there he had the news cried about the streets that the Prince of the Seven Golden Cows was dead, and that he had died rich.

At once the noblemen and the well-to-do merchants and the beggars flocked to the castle. "How sad the news! The good Prince of the Seven Golden Cows, there was no one like him in all the world. For his sake we would have gone through fire and water. Perhaps he has remembered us in his will," they said as they crowded into the courtyard.

Then the door of the castle opened and the Black Steward rode forth, his big cudgel in his hands and his hounds at his horse's heels. "After them! Away with them!" he cried to the hounds. And the hounds ran, biting and snarling, among the noblemen and the merchants and the beggars, whilst the Black Steward laid about him with his cudgel until the courtyard was empty. "Let that be the legacy of the Prince of the Seven Golden Cows," he said.

Then the Black Steward returned to the place where the Prince of the Seven Golden Cows was buried, and he studied and learnt Latin. And when he knew enough Latin to read the prayers in the prayer book, he became a monk; and with the gold from the River Gers he built a monastery, where night and day he prayed for the soul of his master, the Prince of the Seven Golden Cows.

Long before the white men came to America,
the land belonged to the Indians,
and the red men not only cultivated the land
but celebrated everything that lived on it.
They had storytellers who went from camp
to camp. The Ojibways, the Iroquois, the Navahos,
and all the other tribes had tales and legends
as well as fables of their own. Here are four of them.
The first three are retold by Louis Untermeyer,
the fourth by Henry R. Schoolcraft.

# Tales of the American Indians

### RETOLD BY LOUIS UNTERMEYER
### AND HENRY R. SCHOOLCRAFT

## How the Birds Came

WHEN THE Great Spirit made the world, he made it wonderful—wonderful to look at, wonderful to live in. He walked up and down his new creation and, wherever he went, beauty was born. His hands shaped the hills; rivers and lakes sprang up where his feet touched the earth. He breathed, and the ground was covered with flowers; he called, and forests answered him with the sound of a million trees. Man and the animals had not yet come.

Meanwhile, everything was good and glad. The little leaves talked all day long and sang their best when a breeze passed by. The breeze knew that nothing lives forever, and he felt sad when the first summer was over.

But the little leaves were not afraid. They thought that summer would never end, and they continued to sing. They did not mind the chill wind of autumn; they merely changed their dress of green for brighter colors. But soon they trembled with the cold. They could not hold on to the branches and, shivering, they fell to the ground.

The Great Spirit saw them lying there and was sorry for them. He could not alter the law of nature and put them back on the trees—but he could give them a new life, which would let them sing forever. So he gave each leaf a pair of wings.

From the red leaves of the maples came robin redbreasts and cardinals. The yellow birch leaves flew gaily into the sky as orioles, goldfinches, and wild canaries. The dark oak leaves turned into blackbirds, bluejays, and purple martins. Even the most withered brown leaves lived again in little wrens, perky sparrows, and singing thrushes.

That is how the birds came.

187

# How the Woodpecker Was Born

FROM TIME to time the Great Spirit, the Master of Life, roamed the earth to see what was happening to his creations. Calling himself Manito, and disguised as an old man, he went from village to village, talking to men and women as if he were one of them.

One wintry day he came to the wigwam of the head of a tribe. The chief was out hunting, but his wife, dressed in fine clothes, was sitting in front of the fire.

"I have been fasting for days," said Manito, "and I would be grateful for something to eat."

"Well," said the woman, "there is little food here. But I suppose I could bake you a cake, if you could wait."

The Great Spirit knew that she had venison and other rich meat hidden away, but he only said, "I can wait."

Whereupon the woman baked a very small cake. When it had cooked, she looked at it and it seemed quite large. "This is too good for an old man," she thought. "Besides, if he is starving he will be glad to get anything." So she took a little dough and made a much smaller cake.

"The first cake was for my husband," she said untruthfully, "but I will make another for you."

"I can wait," said Manito.

When the second cake was baked it looked almost as large as the first one. "I will keep this for myself," she thought, "for it is a shame to waste anything so good on such an old fellow." So she said to Manito, "This one did not turn out right. I will make one more."

"I can wait," said the Great Spirit.

The third cake was the smallest of them all, but she could not bear to give even this one away. She turned angrily to Manito and said, "You see how little food we have. There is nothing here for you. If you are hungry enough you can search for things to eat in the forest—on bushes and in the bark of trees."

Then Manito shed his disguise and towered above the woman in his own form as the Great Spirit.

"Life has been good to you," he said, "but you are not good to those who need life. You shall no longer live in a warm wigwam with plenty of fine things to eat. You shall live in the forest and search for your food, even in the bark of the trees. You have a small spirit, and you shall have a small body to match your soul."

As he said these words the woman grew smaller and smaller. Her clothes changed into feathers; wings grew from her body; and, with a small cry, she flew out of the wigwam into the forest.

That is how the first woodpecker was born. And that is why all woodpeckers live in the forest and search for their food in the bark of trees.

# How the Hare Got in the Moon

ONCE UPON a time all the animals were at peace with one another. In those days the Fox and the Hare were not enemies but friends. They lived together and helped each other in every possible way.

The Great Spirit was pleased to see so much gentleness and kindness and, wearing his disguise as Manito, he visited the two friends. "May I come in and rest my tired bones?" he asked. "I am weary with walking."

"By all means," said the Fox and the Hare. "We always help each other, and we will be glad to help you."

"Such a welcome is better than food," said Manito. "But I must admit I would like to share a meal with two such generous creatures."

Both the Hare and the Fox hung their heads. "We are ashamed that we have nothing in our lodge fit for a visitor," they said. "Nevertheless, we will try to find something somewhere." And they disappeared into the woods.

When they returned the Fox said, "Alas, I have little to offer. The fruit has fallen from the trees; the berries have been picked; all I could find were some grains of wheat that had not been gathered. With this we can make a little bread."

"But our visitor should have something more nourishing to go with the bread," said the Hare. "I could find nothing except—"

"Except what?" asked the Fox. "Surely you do not know where meat can be found for our visitor!"

"Yes, I do," said the Hare. "Stir up the fire and you shall see."

When the fire had been built up the Hare said, "Although we Hares do not eat flesh, men live on it. So I will throw myself into the fire and offer my flesh for food."

As the Hare sprang toward the fire the Great Spirit caught him in midair and, before the flames could touch him, Manito spoke.

"Unselfish little animal, you have offered the most that anyone could offer —you have offered yourself. I will accept your gift, but not in the way you intended. I will carry you from the earth up to the moon. There you will shine in glory. Everyone will look on you as a token of kindness and unselfishness— something that will stay bright forever."

That is why the Indians see a hare instead of a man in the moon.

# How Corn Came into the World

IN TIMES past a poor Indian lived with his wife and children in a beautiful part of the country. He was not expert at procuring food for his family, and his children were too young to give him much help. His eldest son had now arrived at the proper age to undertake the ceremony of the Ke-ig-uish-im-o-win, or fast, to prove his fitness for manhood, and to see what manner of spirit would be his guide through life.

Wunzh, for this was his name, was an obedient boy beloved by the whole family. When spring came they built him the customary little lodge some distance from their own, where he would not be disturbed during this solemn rite.

He immediately went into the lodge and commenced his fast. The first few days he amused himself by walking in the woods, examining the plants and flowers. In this way he prepared himself to enjoy his sleep, and stored his mind with pleasant thoughts for his dreams.

He felt a strong desire to know how the plants, herbs, and berries grew without any aid from man, and why it was that some species were good to eat, and others possessed medicinal or poisonous juices. He recalled these thoughts after he became too languid to walk about, and wished he could dream of something that would prove a benefit to his family, and to all others.

"True," he thought, "the Great Spirit made all things, and it is to him that we owe our lives. But could he not make it easier for us to get our food than by hunting animals and taking fish? I must try to find out this in my visions."

On the third day he became weak and faint and kept to his bed. He fancied that he saw a handsome young man coming down from the sky and advancing toward him. The young man was richly dressed in garments of green and yellow, but differing in their deeper or lighter shades. He had a waving plume on his head, and all his motions were graceful.

"I am sent to you, my friend," said the celestial visitor, "by that Great Spirit who made all things in the sky and on the earth. He knows your motive in fasting. He sees that it is from a benevolent wish to do good to your people."

He then told the young man to arise and prepare to wrestle with him, as it was only by this means that he could hope to succeed in his wishes. Wunzh was weak from fasting, but he felt courage rising in his heart. Immediately he got up, determined to die rather than fail. He commenced the trial, and after a protracted effort was almost exhausted.

Then the beautiful stranger said, "My friend, it is enough for once; I will come again to try you." Smiling at him, he ascended in the air.

The next day the celestial visitor reappeared and renewed the trial. Wunzh felt that his strength was even less than the day before, but the courage of his mind seemed to increase in proportion as his body became weaker. Seeing this, the stranger said, "Be strong, my friend, for this is the only way you can overcome me and obtain the boon you seek."

On the third day he again appeared and renewed the struggle. The youth

was faint in body, but determined to prevail. He exerted his utmost powers, and after the contest had been continued the usual time, the stranger declared himself conquered. Sitting down beside the youth, he told him in what manner he should proceed to take advantage of his victory.

"You have won your desire of the Great Spirit," said the stranger. "You have wrestled manfully. Tomorrow I shall meet you and wrestle with you for the last time. As soon as you have prevailed against me, you will strip off my garments and throw me down, clean the earth of roots and weeds, make it soft, and bury me in the spot.

"When you have done this, leave my body in the earth. Do not disturb it, but come occasionally to visit the place, to see whether I have come to life. Be careful never to let the grass or weeds grow on my grave. Once a month cover me with fresh earth. If you follow my instructions, you will accomplish your object of doing good to your fellow creatures by teaching them the knowledge I now teach you." He then disappeared.

In the morning the youth's father came with some slight refreshment, saying, "My son, you have fasted long enough. If the Great Spirit will favor you, he will do it now. It is seven days since you have tasted food, and you must not sacrifice your life. The Master of Life does not require that."

"My father," replied the youth, "wait till the sun goes down. I have a particular reason for extending my fast."

At the usual hour of the day the sky visitor returned, and the trial of strength was renewed. Although the youth had not availed himself of his father's offer of food, he grasped his angelic antagonist with supernatural strength, threw him down, and took from him his beautiful garments and plume. Finding him dead, he buried him on the spot, confident that his friend would again come to life.

He then returned to his father's lodge and partook sparingly of the meal that had been prepared for him. But he never forgot the grave of his friend. He visited it throughout the spring, and carefully weeded out the grass and kept the ground in a soft and pliant state. Soon he saw the tops of the green plumes coming through the ground; and the more careful he was to keep the ground in order, the faster they grew.

Days and weeks passed. Summer was drawing toward a close when one day, after a long absence in hunting, Wunzh invited his father to follow him to the quiet spot of his former fast. The lodge had been removed, but in its place stood a tall, graceful plant with bright-colored silken hair, surmounted with nodding plumes and stately leaves, and golden clusters on each side.

"It is my friend," shouted the lad. "It is the friend of all mankind. It is Mondamin."

He then pulled an ear of corn. "See, my father," said he, "this is what I fasted for. The Great Spirit has listened to my voice, and sent us something new. We need no longer rely on hunting alone. As long as this gift is cherished and taken care of, the ground itself will give us a living."

He then communicated to his father the instructions given him by the stranger. The broad husks must be torn away, as he had pulled off the garments in his wrestling. Then the ear must be held before the fire until the outer skin became brown, while all the milk was retained in the grain.

The whole family then united in a feast on the newly grown ears, expressing gratitude to the Merciful Spirit who gave it.

Thus corn came into the world.

# The Water-Sprite and the Bear

### RETOLD BY BARBARA LEONIE PICARD

IN A MILL beside a stream, a short way from a village, lived a miller. He was a cheerful, good-natured man, and would have been contented enough with his lot had it not been for one misfortune. In the stream close by the mill lived a water-sprite, a sly, ugly creature with dank hair like water-weeds, sharp, pointed teeth and flat, webbed feet.

At first it was bad enough when the water-sprite's head would suddenly appear above the water and he would look inquisitively as anyone passed by; but it was worse when he began to climb on to the bank of the stream and sit there, showing his long teeth in a thoughtful grin and watching with his unblinking, pebble-like eyes the miller or his wife, the serving-wench or the boy who helped in the mill.

"He gives me the creeps," said the miller's wife, "sitting there like that."

And the boy said, "He is ugly, and no mistake." But the serving-wench just gave a scream whenever she caught sight of him, picked up her skirts and ran.

Yet all that was nothing to what came later. The miller had had little to grumble about so far. But one day the water-sprite padded up the steps to the mill, put his head round the door, said, "Good morning, miller," in his wet voice and came in and settled himself comfortably on the floor in a corner by the hearth.

The miller was not one to grudge a warm, dry corner to anyone, not even to a water-sprite—the last kind of creature, surely, whom one would expect to want such a thing—but the water-sprite took to coming into the mill whenever it pleased him, at any hour of the day or night, and prowling around for all the world as though it were his own place,

197

so that, just when one least expected him, there he would be: under the table at supper time, waiting in the kitchen the first thing in the morning, padding behind one on his silent feet when one had supposed oneself to be alone, or appearing suddenly at a dark turn of the stairs just as one was going to bed. Or perhaps the very worst of all was when, after an evening in which he had—most happily—failed to appear at all, he would be found curled up asleep in the middle of the bed, lying on a patch of damp bedclothes, for, of course, he always dripped stream water wherever he went.

In a few weeks he was quite at home in the mill, and one could be sure of meeting him there at least once every day. By this time the serving-wench had left—running all the way home to the village one night after finding the water-sprite on the stairs in the dark—and her place had been taken by no fewer than three others, each of whom had, in turn, quickly followed her example, and the miller's wife was having to do all her own work.

One evening, the water-sprite showed great interest while the miller's wife was cooking the supper, coming quite close

and sniffing at the roasting meat. The next morning he arrived at breakfast time, carrying a fish on the end of a stick. He sat himself down by the hearth and broiled his fish over the fire. When it was cooked, he tasted it cautiously, liked what he tasted and ate it up in two bites. After that he always cooked his meals at the hearth, four or five fish at breakfast and supper, and scrunched them up, heads and tails and bones and all, with his long teeth, watching the miller and his wife thoughtfully as he did so, in a manner which they found most disconcerting. It quite put them off their own meals.

Another pretty trick of his was to set the mill wheel racing in the middle of the night, so that the miller and his wife would wake up in a fright, and the miller would have to get up and go to see what was the matter.

It was, of course, inevitable, with such a state of affairs, that there should come a day when the miller found himself alone in the mill. Not a single girl from the village would come to work for him, his boy's father had found the lad another master, and his wife had gone home to her mother. So the miller was all alone—all alone, that is, save for the water-sprite. But because the mill was his livelihood and had been his home as well for all his life, he had to stay on, in company with the water-sprite; and little comfort he found in such a companion.

One evening, just after dark, a bear-ward knocked on the door of the mill and asked lodging for the night. He was on his way from one village to another with his dancing bear. The miller sighed, for he dearly liked a good evening's talk and he saw little enough of other folk these days, and the bearward looked a cheerful fellow with a merry grin and a bright eye, a man, indeed, after the miller's own heart.

"It is unlike me to be inhospitable," said the miller. "Not so long ago I never dreamt there would come a day when I would turn a stranger from my door at night. The village is only a few miles on, my friend, you had best go there, to the inn." And he told the bearward about the water-sprite. "It is all I can do, to stay here myself," he said. "A hundred times a week I tell myself, 'Tomorrow I shall lock the door and throw the key in the stream and go.' But I always manage just one day more. Yet one cannot expect a stranger to put up with it."

"I am not afraid of a water-sprite," said the bearward with a chuckle. "But I have walked a long way today, and I have no mind to walk even a few miles more. I am tired, and so is Braun here." He jerked a thumb over his shoulder towards the shaggy brown bear on the end of a chain.

"Very well," said the miller, "come in, and most welcome you will be. But never say I did not warn you." He stood aside to let the bearward through. "You had best bring your bear in with you; you never know what may happen to him if you leave him in the barn."

The bearward laughed. "Braun can take care of himself. He would make short work of any water-sprite, I warrant. Just you let us have a sight of this plague of yours and we may be able to do you a service, Braun and I."

The water-sprite had already had his supper and gone back to the stream, so the two men had a pleasant evening together, chatting of this and that, and since the water-sprite did not appear again before they went to bed, to the miller it seemed quite like old times, and he began to feel more cheerful than he had felt for months.

The miller and his guest shared the big bedroom, with the bear curled up on the floor beside the bed; and there was no sign of the water-sprite all night.

They got up early in the morning and went down to the kitchen for their breakfast, the bear coming after them. But, early as they were, the water-sprite was earlier. There he was, sitting by the hearth, the embers raked together to make a good fire for him to cook his breakfast on, and four broiled fishes laid out on the floor beside him in a row, ready for him to eat when he had cooked the fifth.

The miller's face fell, and the morning suddenly seemed not so bright and pleasant after all. "There he is," he whispered miserably.

The water-sprite looked up, showed his teeth and, "Good morning, miller," he said. He gave one glance at the stranger, saw nothing to interest him there, and went on with the cooking of his last fish.

The bearward watched him for a moment; then he turned to the miller, winked, and called back over his shoulder, "Come on, Braun, here is your breakfast for you. Look, good fish." He pointed, gave the bear a push, and the bear ambled towards the hearth, sniffed at the fishes laid out on the floor, liked what it smelt, picked one up and swallowed it in one bite—one bite more quickly than the water-sprite could have managed. Before the water-sprite realized what was happening, the bear had taken a second helping; but before it could manage a third, the water-sprite had jumped to his feet, quite furious, and was shaking his fists at the bear. "Away with you! Away with you, you thieving creature!"

The bear sat up and looked at the water-sprite, but made no attempt to go away. Instead, after a moment, it made a move to take the third fish.

"My fish! My fish!" screamed the water-sprite, beside himself with rage. And he rushed at the bear to drive it away.

The bear put out a great paw and clouted the water-sprite, who shrieked and turned tail, making for the mill door and his stream as fast as he could, followed by the growling bear. At the door the bear turned and came back for the remaining three fishes, which it ate happily by the fire, while the miller, delighted with the way things had turned out, made the breakfast.

The bearward laughed loudly. "Well," he said, "did I or did I not tell you that Braun would make short work of any water-sprite?"

After breakfast the bearward went on his way to the village and the miller began his work, feeling happier than he had felt for a very long time. In fact, he felt so happy that he sang at his work, a thing he had long forgotten to do.

All that day the water-sprite never showed himself near the mill, and it was the same the next day, and the next, for nearly a week; and the miller was feel-

ing on top of the world and thinking of taking a day off from work the very next morning and going over to his wife's mother's house to tell his wife to come home, when, coming whistling into the kitchen for supper, he saw the water-sprite sitting by the hearth cooking his fish.

The miller could have wept. Now it would start all over again, he thought. No wife, no boy to help him, no serving-wench, no peace in the mill, ever again.

"Good evening, miller," said the water-sprite, showing his long teeth. But the miller had not even the heart to give him a civil answer—though he usually did, just in case the water-sprite took offence: one never knew, and it was al-

ways best to be on the safe side, with those long teeth.

The miller sat down at the table, too miserable to trouble about getting himself any supper. After a time the water-sprite said, "That big cat of yours with the long claws, miller; I have not seen it for several days. Has it gone away?"

For a moment the miller went on staring at the table top, thinking regretfully of the bear, not even finding the idea of a bear-sized cat amusing, though it would once have made him laugh. Then suddenly his heart gave a great bound, for he was really quite a quick-witted man. He looked up and said, as casually as he could, "Why no! She has just had kittens. You will be seeing her around

again soon, and all the seven little ones with her. They are just like their mother, only smaller. But they will soon grow. They will soon grow."

The water-sprite looked at the miller with his round, pebbly eyes even rounder than usual, if that were possible. Then he dropped the fish he was cooking and sprang up. "Is that so? Seven little ones?" he said with a shriek. "Then I am off! Good-bye, miller, you will not be seeing me again." And he was away out of the mill as fast as his flat feet could carry him, and into the water and down the stream and away for good and all.

And the miller never set eyes on him again.

# Favorite Funny Limericks

## BY EDWARD LEAR

There was a young lady whose chin
Resembled the point of a pin;
   So she had it made sharp
   And purchased a harp
And played several tunes with her chin.

There was an old man who supposed
That the street door was partially closed.
   But some very large rats
   Ate his coats and his hats
While that silly old gentleman dozed.

There was a young lady whose nose
Was so long that it reached to her toes.
   So she hired a lady
   Whose conduct was steady
To carry that wonderful nose.

There was an old man who said, "How
Shall I flee from this horrible cow?
   I will sit on this stile
   And continue to smile,
Which may soften the heart of that cow."

There was an old man of the coast
Who placidly sat on a post.
   But when it turned cold
   He relinquished his hold
And called for some hot buttered toast.

There was an old man of Cape Horn
Who wished he had never been born;
   So he sat on a chair
   Till he died of despair,
That dolorous man of Cape Horn.

There was an old man with a beard
Who said, "It is just as I feared!
   Two owls and a hen,
   Four larks and a wren,
Have all built their nests in my beard!"

There was a young lady in blue
Who said, "Is it you? Is it you?"
   When they said, "Yes, it is,"
   She replied only, "Whizz!"
That ungracious lady in blue.

*The history of the foolish boy*
*who never can figure out the right thing to do*
*has been told many times in many different ways*
*in many countries.*
*You can find it in Germany, in France,*
*in the Far East, and in America.*
*This version, "Lazy Jack,"*
*comes from England.*

# Lazy Jack

## BY FLORA ANNIE STEEL

ONCE upon a time there was a boy whose name was Jack, and he lived with his mother on a common. They were very poor, and the old woman got her living by spinning, but Jack was so lazy that he would do nothing but bask in the sun in the hot weather, and sit by the corner of the hearth in the winter-time. So they called him Lazy Jack. His mother could not get him to do anything for her, and at last told him one Monday, that if he did not begin to work for his porridge she would turn him out to get his living as he could.

This roused Jack, and he went out and hired himself for the next day to a neighboring farmer for a penny; but as he was coming home, never having had any money before, he lost it in passing over a brook.

"You stupid boy," said his mother, "you should have put it in your pocket."

"I'll do so another time," replied Jack.

Well, the next day, Jack went out again and hired himself to a cowkeeper, who gave him a jar of milk for his day's work. Jack took the jar and put it into the large pocket of his jacket, spilling it all, long before he got home.

"Dear me!" said the old woman; "you should have carried it on your head."

"I'll do so another time," said Jack.

So the following day, Jack hired himself again to a farmer, who agreed to give him a cream cheese for his services. In the evening Jack took the cheese, and went home with it on his head. By the time he got home the cheese was all spoilt, part of it being lost, and part matted with his hair.

"You stupid lout," said his mother, "you should have carried it very carefully in your hands."

"I'll do so another time," replied Jack.

Now the next day, Lazy Jack again went out, and hired himself to a baker, who would give him nothing for his work but a large tom-cat. Jack took the cat, and began carrying it very carefully in his hands, but in a short time pussy scratched him so much that he was compelled to let it go.

When he got home, his mother said to him, "You silly fellow, you should have tied it with a string, and dragged it along after you."

"I'll do so another time," said Jack.

So on the following day, Jack hired himself to a butcher, who rewarded him by the handsome present of a shoulder of mutton. Jack took the mutton, tied it to a string, and trailed it along after him in the dirt, so that by the time he had got home the meat was completely spoilt. His mother was this time quite out of patience with him, for the next day was Sunday, and she was obliged to do with cabbage for her dinner.

"You ninney-hammer," said she to her son; "you should have carried it on your shoulder."

"I'll do so another time," replied Jack.

Well, on the Monday, Lazy Jack went once more, and hired himself to a cattle-keeper, who gave him a donkey for his trouble. Now though Jack was strong he found it hard to hoist the donkey on his shoulders, but at last he did it, and began walking home slowly with his prize. Now it so happened that in the course of his journey he passed a house where a rich man lived with his only daughter, a beautiful girl, who was deaf and dumb. And she had never laughed in her life,

and the doctors said she would never speak till somebody made her laugh. So the father had given out that any man who made her laugh would receive her hand in marriage.

Now this young lady happened to be looking out of the window when Jack was passing by with the donkey on his shoulders; and the poor beast with its legs sticking up in the air was kicking violently and hee-hawing with all its might. Well, the sight was so comical that she burst out into a great fit of laughter, and immediately recovered her speech and hearing. Her father was overjoyed, and fulfilled his promise by marrying her to Lazy Jack, who was thus made a rich gentleman. They lived in a large house, and Jack's mother lived with them in great happiness until the day she died.

*Most of the stories in this book are of
an earlier time and of another world.
This story however takes place in the world
in which we live...in fact, in the house in which we live—
or one very much like it.
Animals live here, too; in particular one small brown mouse
and one large fearsome cat.
But on a certain night, everything changes—
everything is different—and the mouse has nothing to fear.*

# The Small Brown Mouse

BY JANET MCNEILL

YOU MIGHT not think that smells would travel round the corners in a mousehole, but you would be wrong. The small brown mouse knows at exactly what angle in the hole to sit so that all the smells from the room beyond are reflected to him, accurately and deliciously. He is safe there, with the roof of the mousehole just above his head, and the

sides of it sitting snugly to his shoulders, so that nothing can jump at him suddenly from any direction, and he can see the light from the room shining up the tunnel which generations of his family have polished with their furry flanks. Whichever of his ancestors it was who had been the architect for that mousehole, he had known his business well, and each evening the small brown mouse takes up his position, and his quivering nose-tip explores all the smells that reach him.

In the winter evenings the most exciting of the smells are of cocoa and digestive biscuits. And when he smells those the small brown mouse knows that soon there will be a stir in the room, chairs will be pushed back, someone will say, "Come on, puss—time you were out," doors will open and shut again, feet will sound on the stairs, light feet first, then heavier feet, and at last the room will be left in the quiet dark, but for the glimmer from what is left of the fire.

This is the moment that the mouse has been waiting for. He comes out of the mousehole and across the floor like the flicker of a shadow, and he has his supper from the crumbs on the carpet, and he is thankful that digestive biscuits are so very brittle, and that the family make so many crumbs.

One evening in the middle of winter, the small brown mouse was sitting just round his particular angle in the mousehole, waiting for his supper. It was cold and frosty outside, and he was hungry, and he hoped the biscuits had been rather more brittle than usual, and the family more careless. He waited and he waited, growing hungrier and hungrier, but also more and more puzzled. For mixed up with the smell of cocoa and digestive biscuits he smelt other, unfamiliar smells, which greatly puzzled even so wise a mouse as he. There was cigarette smoke, of course, and the smell of the fire, and he rather thought someone had been sucking peppermints. But there was a very unusual smell—unusual, that is, for a drawingroom—a fresh keen

outdoor smell, a smell that didn't belong to a house at all, and there were other sweeter smells that were foreign to him, and most exciting.

The small feet had gone up to bed a long time ago. The other, heavier feet should have been on their way, but still the light burned and there came the continued sound of voices. What with hunger and curiosity the small brown mouse crept another inch towards the room—and then crept an inch back again, for the cat was still there, the silent presence that turned your legs to water and made your heart sick, the dreadful and inescapable cat.

The mouse was beginning to think he should go back up the mousehole and take his supper off the piece of cheese-rind he had stored there, in case of emergencies, when at last he heard the familiar sounds that he had been waiting for. Chairs scraped across the floor, the cat was called, the front door opened and closed again, the light was extinguished and feet—slow, tired feet—went up the stairs.

The small brown mouse came out of the mousehole and looked around him. And he forgot all about the digestive biscuits, but sat back on his little haunches, and with bright unwinking eyes he stared his fill.

It was a tree, a tall strong tree, set in a tub at the further end of the room. That was the outdoor smell, though what a tree was doing inside a house the mouse did not know. But he breathed in the sharp sweet smell of its branches, and it reminded him of the wood where, in the sunny summertime, he had sometimes wandered. But this tree was differ-

ent from all other trees. Its dark green branches were hung and spattered from tip to toe. It burned and glittered and sparkled. It was alive with bright colours that were not fruit nor blossom. And at the top was a figure, half child, half bird, and he knew that it was an angel.

Forgetting how hungry he was the mouse crept forward to investigate this unexpected tree. He climbed carefully over the tub and up among the branches, nosing around backward and forward, smelling and feeling and looking at all the things that he found there. There was a bottle of French perfume, and though it was tightly wrapped and stoppered, his nose discovered it, and it made him feel very romantic and sentimental so that he nearly ran away home up the mousehole, to tell his wife about it right away. But a little higher up there was a cigar, and although there was only a breath of it coming through its silvery case, it was enough to make our mouse feel bold and manly, so that he went higher up still, examining everything as he went.

There were boxes of chocolates and trumpets, balls and oranges, candles, wisps of tinsel, cotton wool snow, tiny shining birds that dipped on the branches as his small weight came on to them, and flaunted bright glittering tails. There were books and boxes of handkerchiefs, and many other things which baffled the mouse completely, so strange and unusual they were. But what he most admired were the large bright balls, red and blue, green and gold, in which, by the light of the fire, he could see his own reflection looking out at him—a warlike red mouse in the red ball, a romantic blue mouse, a mermaid mouse of cool translucent green. Best of all was an amber ball which reflected a tawny benevolent lion of a mouse, a mouse as truly golden as the cheese that mice dream about when they are happiest.

Soon he had been all over the tree, except for the highest branches, where there was little foothold, and where even his feather weight might find little enough support. It was only then that he remembered how hungry he was, and he went down to the carpet again, and ate up the crumbs of the digestive biscuits, and as he chewed he never took his eyes off the splendid tree.

His supper gave him courage, and he decided that after all he would attempt the last perilous inches to the top, where on the slender stem the angel was poised.

So up he went again, scrambling and sliding, and he paused only to look just once more at his golden self, reflected in the amber glass ball. And at last there was only a slim six inches between him and the small white feet of the angel.

But just at the base of the final pinnacle was something that the mouse had not seen in his first excursion, something as small as himself, something in fact very like himself—three chocolate mice. They lay side by side on the very last branch, just beneath the angel, and our mouse looked at them, first with curiosity and then with pity, for they were clumsy things compared with his own exquisite shape. Their ears were no more than humps on either side of their thick heads; their eyes were just spots of white sugar on the chocolate—set on unevenly at that; there wasn't a whisker between

210

them; and their tails were poor things of limp string that hung down behind them. Our mouse looked back at his own elegant tapered tail that kept the balance of his body, and he looked again at the dangling bits of string, and he felt rather ashamed. But he also felt extremely interested, for the smell of the chocolate had reached him so suddenly and so magnificently that he almost lost his balance and fell from his precarious perch.

It was like the smell of cocoa, of course, but so much better, so much richer, that there was really little comparison. The shock of its sweetness paralysed him for a moment, and then he came a little closer, delaying—just for the pure pleasure of delaying—the lovely moment when his tongue should slide up the shining sides of the first mouse.

"No," said the angel suddenly—so suddenly that the small brown mouse once more had difficulty in keeping his footing

—"No. Not now—not yet—not for you."

She wasn't scolding, she was just telling him, and she smiled at him as she spoke so that the mouse was at once ashamed of himself. "Yes ma'am," he said, and because the chocolate mice still smelt so overpoweringly beautiful—so much so that he could not keep his whiskers from vibrating—he came down off the tree, where the smell of them was mixed up with a lot of other smells, and he finished up a few crumbs of biscuit that he had previously overlooked.

He should then have gone back into the safety of his mousehole, but he could not bring himself to leave the enchanted tree, and all night he sat in front of the fire, watching it.

Even when the last flicker of the fire had burned itself out, and the coals sighed and fell together in white ash on the hearth, the mouse still sat on, for of course a mouse can see in the dark, and this mouse had never seen anything like this before. He forgot his wife who was waiting for him, he forgot to count the hours striking on the big clock in the hall, he forgot everything except the tree. That was why, when morning had come he was still sitting there when the mistress of the house opened the door—and the cat walked in! Before he knew it the great cat was coming softly and steadily across the hearth towards him, and the mouse knew that he was lost indeed.

The cat sat down placidly, a few feet away, and made no spring. The mouse watched him, sick with fear, unable to move. He wished the cat would be quick and spring, and make a finish to it.

"Hallo, nipper," said the great animal,

and the mouse saw his strong white pointed teeth as he spoke; "don't be in a hurry to move. You needn't mind me."

And still he didn't spring.

"I'm not going to chase you," the cat said. And for some reason that he could not explain the mouse believed the cat, just as he had believed the angel.

"Why not?" he asked, trying to keep the wobble out of his voice.

"I don't know exactly," the cat replied, blinking a mild yellow eye, "but it's a

thing we always do at this time of year. Traditional, you know."

The mouse didn't know, but a warm gratitude made it impossible for him to speak.

"Mind you," the cat went on, "I shall chase you to-morrow, and every other day that I get the chance. Like as not I shall catch you too. But not today." And he busied himself licking the pads of his great paws, keeping the claws politely hooded.

The mouse believed this too. He knew that the cat would indeed chase him to-morrow and every other day, but he also knew that after this it would always be different. He would be able to run away from the cat now, because he knew that the cat was just another animal, as he himself was an animal — a much stronger animal of course, but just an animal: not a horror that turned your legs to water and made your heart sick. Oh yes, he could run away from the cat now. Out of sheer bravado he crept across the few feet that lay between the cat and himself, and he leaned for a small daring moment against the cat's side, and felt the warmth and power of his great body. That would be something to tell his wife about when he got home.

Then the house began to stir, there were laughter and voices, people came and went, the cat was called for his breakfast—and the small brown mouse, who was by this time so excited that he hardly knew what he was doing, instead of running to his mousehole and safety, streaked for the tree, and lay hidden among its branches and saw all that was going on.

There was plenty to see. Visitors arrived all day long. They greeted each

other, and laughed, and opened parcels, and kissed, and sang. And in the evening they drew the curtains across the windows, and they lighted the candles on the tree.

This was something so alarming that the mouse, between the striking of one match and the next, fled up the tree where there were no candles, and found himself lying once again beside his chocolate cousins.

When all the candles were lit, the parcels were untied from the tree, and handed down into small excited hands, and the mouse, from his point of vantage, looked down on the children's upturned faces. Then it was the turn for the grown-up people to receive their parcels, and at last each pair of hands was filled.

There was nothing left on the tree

now, except the angel and the candles and the bright balls—oh, and the chocolate mice. "I'd forgotten about these," someone said, and a hand reached up and up, among the branches.

There was no hope for it—he would be discovered. But just as the fingers fumbled for the chocolate mice, the angel's golden wing tilted ever so slightly, and the small brown mouse was safely sheltered behind it. There he lay, hidden and safe, until the party was over, until people had said good-bye, until the door had opened many times and shut again, until the candles were blown out and the light extinguished, and until the last of the feet had once more gone up the stairs and the house was quiet.

Suddenly it all seemed rather sad. Even the tree looked a little sad. The mouse thought of all the hands that had gone home full of treasures, and he felt sad, too—sad, and also tremendously tired.

"I'll go now," he said to the angel, "and thank you, ma'am, for helping me."

And he got slowly down off the tree—he was stiff with lying so long in one position—and he crossed the room to the mousehole. Just before he went home he turned to the tree, for one last look.

"You are sad," the angel said. "What is the matter?"

He found it difficult to explain. "You said 'Not yet—not now'," he faltered, "but the party is over."

Just then the amber ball slid off the twig that held it, softly down from one branch to another, gently to the ground, and it rolled to his feet and stopped there.

The mouse looked up at the angel questioningly. "For me?" And the angel smiled and nodded.

You might not think that a bright ball from a Christmas tree would travel round the corners in a mousehole. But you would be wrong.

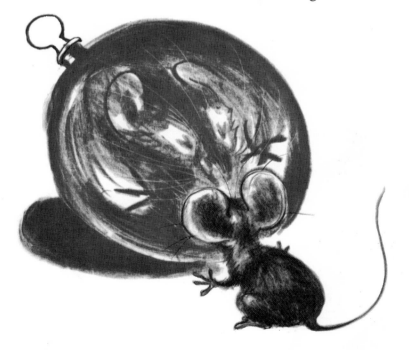

*You might think that a book called*
The Little Old Woman Who Used Her Head
*was about someone who*
*planned things very carefully*
*and did only what was very sensible.*
*On the contrary, the little old woman never did anything*
*sensible and used her head for the silliest schemes.*
*But, as far as she was concerned,*
*her daffiness worked very well…*
*as you will see.*

## *From*
# The Little Old Woman
# Who Used Her Head

### BY HOPE NEWELL

### HOW SHE FINISHED HER RED MUFFLER

THE Little Old Woman was very poor. If she had not been so clever, she probably could not have made both ends meet. But she was a great one for using her head.

One warm summer morning the Little Old Woman looked out of the door of her little yellow house. She said to herself:

"It is too hot to work in my soup garden today. I will sit down by the window and knit myself a red muffler."

So she took her yarn and knitting needles out of the bureau drawer and put on her spectacles. Then she sat down by the window and began to knit herself a red muffler.

Pretty soon the Little Old Woman's

217

geese wanted to go swimming in a pond not far from the house. They went to the gate and flapped their wings. "Honk, honk!" they said.

The Little Old Woman got up and put her yarn and knitting needles away in the drawer and took off her spectacles. She went out and opened the gate so the geese could go to the pond.

When all the geese were out of the yard, the Little Old Woman closed the gate and came back to the house. She took her yarn and knitting needles out of the bureau drawer and put on her spectacles. Then she sat down by the window and went on knitting her red muffler.

She had hardly knitted a dozen stitches before the geese came back from the pond. They stood outside the gate flapping their wings and shaking the water off their backs.

"Honk, honk!" they said.

The Little Old Woman got up again. She put her yarn and knitting needles away in the bureau drawer and took off her spectacles. She went out and opened the gate.

When all the geese were back in the yard, the Little Old Woman closed the gate and came back to the house. She took her yarn and knitting needles out of the drawer and put on her spectacles. Then she sat down by the window and went on knitting her red muffler.

She had hardly knitted a dozen stitches before the geese wanted to go swimming in the pond again. But the Little Old Woman had no sooner let them out of the gate before they wanted to come back in again.

"Dear me," said the Little Old Woman,

"I am spending all my time letting the geese in and out of the gate. At this rate, I shall never get my red muffler done. I think I will use my head and find out what to do."

So she tied a wet towel around her head and sat down with her forefinger against her nose and shut her eyes.

She used her head and used her head, and after a while she found out what to do.

"I will saw two holes at the bottom of the gate," said the Little Old Woman.

"When the geese want to go to the pond, they can crawl out through one hole. When they come back from the pond after their swim, they can crawl in through the other hole."

So the Little Old Woman fetched her saw and sawed two holes at the bottom of the gate. As she was coming back to the house, she thought:

"Now I will not have to go out to open the gate for the geese. And I shall have my red muffler knitted in no time. What a clever Old Woman I am!"

She took her yarn and knitting needles

out of the bureau drawer and put on her spectacles. Then she sat down by the window and went on with her knitting.

Pretty soon the geese wanted to go swimming in the pond. They went to the gate and flapped their wings.

"Honk, honk!" they said.

But the Little Old Woman did not get up. She sat by the window, knitting her red muffler.

The geese flapped their wings again.

"Honk, honk!" they said.

After a while, the old gander spied one of the holes in the gate. He crawled through the hole and went to the pond. Soon the gray goose spied the hole in the gate, and she crawled through it and went to the pond. Before long, all the other geese spied the hole in the gate, and they crawled through it and went to the pond.

The Little Old Woman sat by the window knitting her red muffler. She had hardly knitted a dozen stitches before the geese came back from the pond.

"Now they will flap their wings and say, 'Honk, honk!'" said the Little Old Woman. "But I will not get up and open the gate. By and by they will find the other hole and crawl through it."

But the geese did not flap their wings and say, "Honk, honk!" And instead of looking for the other hole, every one of them crawled back in the same way they had crawled out.

"How silly the geese are!" said the Little Old Woman. "Here I have made two holes, and they only use one of them. I might have spared myself all the trouble I went to of making the other hole."

All morning long, the Little Old Woman sat by the window and knitted her red muffler. All morning long, the geese crawled back and forth through the same hole in the gate.

At last the Little Old Woman finished the red muffler. But the geese were still crawling back and forth through the same hole in the gate.

"It was very clever of me to make two holes after all," said the Little Old Woman. "The geese will have that hole worn out in no time. When it is worn out, the other hole will come in very handy. What a clever Old Woman I am."

## How She Kept Her Geese Warm

One cold winter night, the Little Old Woman was out in the barn putting her geese to bed. She gave them some corn and took off their little red coats. Then she brushed each little coat with a whisk-broom and carefully shook out the wrinkles.

As she was folding the coats in a neat pile, she thought:

"My poor geese must be very cold at night. I have my cozy fire and my feather bed. But they have not even a blanket to keep them warm."

After the geese had eaten their corn, they began to go to roost.

"Honk, honk!" said the big gander, and he hopped up on the roost.

"Honk, honk!" said the gray goose, and she hopped up on the roost.

"Honk, honk!" said all the other geese, and they hopped up on the roost.

Then the Little Old Woman closed the barn door and went into the house. When she went to bed, she lay awake worrying about the geese. After a while she said to herself:

"I cannot sleep a wink for thinking how cold the geese must be. I had better bring them in the house where it is warm."

So the Little Old Woman dressed herself and went out to the barn to fetch the geese. She shooed them off the roost and put on their little red coats. She picked up two geese, and tucking one under each arm, she carried them into the house.

Then she went out to the barn and

picked up two more geese. She tucked one goose under each arm and carried them into the house.

When the Little Old Woman had brought all the geese into the house, she said to herself:

"Now I must get them ready for bed again."

She took off their little red coats and gave the geese some corn. Then she brushed each little coat with a whisk-broom and carefully shook out all the wrinkles.

As she was folding the coats in a neat pile, she thought:

"It was very clever of me to bring the geese into the house. Now they will be warm, and I shall be able to sleep."

Then the Little Old Woman undressed herself again and went to bed.

After the geese had eaten their corn, they began to roost.

"Honk, honk!" said the gander, and he hopped upon the foot of the Little Old Woman's bed.

"Honk, honk!" said the gray goose, and she hopped up on the foot of the Little Old Woman's bed.

"Honk, honk!" said all the other geese, and they tried to hop up on the foot of the Little Old Woman's bed.

But it was not a very big bed, and there was not enough room for all the geese to roost. They began to fight. They pushed and shoved each other. They hissed and squawked and flapped their wings.

All night long the geese pushed and shoved each other. All night long they hissed and squawked and flapped their wings.

They made so much noise that the Little Old Woman did not sleep a wink.

"This will never do," she said. "When they were in the barn, I did not sleep for thinking how cold they must be. When they are in the house, I cannot sleep because they make so much noise. Perhaps if I use my head, I shall know what to do."

The Little Old Woman tied a wet towel around her forehead. Then she sat down with her forefinger against her nose and shut her eyes.

She used her head and used her head, and after a while she knew what to do.

"I will move the roost into the house,"

221

she said. "The geese will have the cozy fire to keep them warm. Then I will move my bed out into the barn. My feather bed will keep me warm, and I will not be worrying about the geese. They will not keep me awake with their noise. I shall sleep very comfortably in the barn."

The Little Old Woman moved the roost into the house, and she moved her bed out into the barn.

When night came again, she brought the geese into the house. After she had fed them some corn, she took off their little red coats. Then they all hopped up on the roost, and the Little Old Woman went out to the barn to sleep.

Her feather bed kept her as warm as toast. She was not worried about the geese, because she knew that they were warm too. So she slept as sound as a top all night long.

*Here is a story of mistakes.*

*Everyone in it is mistaken, and one mistake leads to another.*

*It all starts when a little girl confuses the south-west part of*

*Great Britain (the part called Wales) with the giant*

*sea-creatures known as whales. This a ridiculous error.*

*But there are times when the ridiculous may be rewarding.*

# Living in W'ales

## BY RICHARD HUGHES

ONCE there was a man who said he didn't like the sort of houses people lived in, so he built a model village. It was not really like a model village at all, because the houses were all big enough for real people to live in, and he went about telling people to come and live in W'ales.

There was also living in Liverpool a little girl who was very nice. So when all the people went off with the man to live in W'ales, she went with them. But the man walked so fast that presently some of them got left behind. The ones who were left behind were the little girl, and an Alsatian dog, and a very cross old lady in a bonnet and black beads, who was all stiff, but had a nice husband, who was left behind too.

So they went along till they came to the sea; and in the sea was a whale. The little girl said, "That was what he meant, I suppose, when he talked about living in W'ales. I expect the others are inside: or, if not, they are in another one. We had better get in this one."

So they shouted to know if they might come in, but the whale didn't hear them. The nice husband said that if that was what living in W'ales meant, he would rather go back to Liverpool; but the horrid old lady said, "Nonsense! I will go and whisper in its ear."

But she was very silly, and so instead of whispering in its ear she went and tried to whisper in its blowhole. Still the whale didn't hear; so she got very cross and said, "None of this nonsense, now! Let us in at once! I won't have it, do you hear? I simply won't stand it!" and she began to stir in his blowhole with her umbrella.

So the whale blew, like an enormous sneeze, and blew her right away up into the sky on top of the water he blew out of his hole, and she was never seen again. So then the nice husband went quietly back to Liverpool.

But the little girl went to the whale's real ear, which was very small and not a bit like his blowhole, and whispered into it, "Please, nice whale, we would so like to come in, if we may, and live inside." Then the whale opened his huge mouth, and the little girl and the Alsatian dog went in.

When they got right down inside, of course, there was no furniture. "He was quite right," said the little girl. "It is certainly not a bit like living in a house."

The only thing in there was a giant's wig that the whale had once eaten. So the little girl said, "This will do for a doormat." So she made it into a doormat, and the Alsatian dog went to sleep on it.

When he woke up again he started to

dig holes; and, of course, it gave the whale most terrible pains to have holes dug by such a big dog in his inside, so he went up to the top of the water and shouted to the Captain of a ship to give him a pill. On board the ship there was a cold dressed leg of mutton that the Captain was tired of, so he thought, "That will make a splendid pill to give the whale." So he threw it to the whale, and the whale swallowed it; and when it came tobogganing down the whale's throat the Alsatian dog, who was very hungry, ate it, and stopped digging holes; and when the dog stopped digging holes the whale's pain went away. So he said "Thank you" to the Captain. "That was an excellent pill."

The Captain was very surprised that his pill had made the whale well again so soon; he had really done it only to get rid of the cold mutton.

But the poor little girl wasn't so lucky as the Alsatian dog. *He* had a doormat to sleep on, and something to eat. But there was no bed, and the little girl couldn't possibly sleep without a bed to sleep on; and she had nothing to eat—and this went on for days and days.

Meanwhile the whale began to get rather worried about them. He had swallowed them without thinking much about it; but he soon began to wonder what was happening to them, and whether they were comfortable. He knew nothing at all about little girls. He thought she would probably want something to eat by now, but he didn't know at all what. So he tried to talk down into his own inside, to ask her. But that is very difficult; at any rate, *he* couldn't do it. The words all came out instead of going in.

225

So he swam off to the tropics, where he knew a parrot, and asked him what to do. The parrot said it was quite simple, and flew off to an island where there was a big snake. He bit off its head and bit off its tail, and then flew back to the whale with the rest of it. He put most of the snake down the whale's throat, so that one end just came up out of its mouth.

"There," he said, "now you have a

speaking tube. You speak into one end of the snake, and the words will go down it inside you."

So the whale said "Hello" into one end of the snake, and the little girl heard "Hello" come out of the other. "What do you want?" said the whale. "I want something to eat," said the little girl. The whale told the parrot, "She wants something to eat. What do little girls eat?"

"Little girls eat rice pudding," said the parrot. He had one, in a big glass bowl; so he poured it down the snake too, and it came down the other end and the little girl ate it.

When she had eaten it she caught hold of her end of the snake, and called

"Hello!" up it. "Hello!" said the whale.

"May I have a bed?" said the little girl.

"She wants a bed," the whale said to the parrot.

"You go to Harrod's for that," said the parrot, "which is the biggest shop in London," and flew away.

When the whale got to Harrod's, he went inside. One of the shopwalkers came

up to him and said, "What can I do for *you*, please?" which sounded very silly.

"I want a bed," said the whale.

"Mr. Binks, BEDS!" The shopwalker called out very loud, and then ran away. He was terribly frightened, because there had never been a whale in the shop before.

Mr. Binks the Bed Man came up and looked rather worried.

"I don't know that we have got a bed that will exactly fit you, sir," he said.

"Why not, silly?" said the whale. "I only want an ordinary one."

"Yes, sir," said the Bed Man, "but it will have to be rather a large ordinary one, won't it?"

"Of course not, silly," said the whale. "On the contrary, it will have to be rather a small one."

He saw a very nice little one standing in a corner.

"I think that one will just about fit me," he said.

"You can have it if you like," said the Bed Man. "But I think it's you who are the silly to think a little bed like that will fit you!"

"I want it to fit me *inside*, of course," said the whale, "not *outside!* . . . Push!" and he opened his mouth.

So they all came and pushed, and sure enough it just did fit him. Then he ate all the pillows and blankets he could find, which was far more than was needed really, and when it all got down inside, the little girl made the bed and went to sleep on it.

So the whale went back to the sea. Now that the little girl and the Alsatian dog both had had something to eat and somewhere to sleep, they said:

"The man was right, it really is much more fun living in W'ales than living in houses."

So they stayed on.

P.S. The parrot went on feeding them, not always on rice pudding.

# The Mock Turtle's Song

### BY LEWIS CARROLL

"Will you walk a little faster?" said a whiting to a snail.
"There's a porpoise close behind us, and he's treading on my tail.
See how eagerly the lobsters and the turtles all advance!
They are waiting on the shingle—will you come and join the dance?
 Will you, won't you, will you, won't you, will you join the dance?
 Will you, won't you, will you, won't you, won't you join the dance?

"You can really have no notion how delightful it will be
When they take us up and throw us, with the lobsters, out to sea!"
But the snail replied, "Too far, too far!" and gave a look askance—
Said he thanked the whiting kindly, but he would not join the dance.
 Would not, could not, would not, could not, would not join the dance.
 Would not, could not, would not, could not, could not join the dance.

"What matters it how far we go?" his scaly friend replied.
"There is another shore, you know, upon the other side.
The further off from England the nearer is to France—
Then turn not pale, beloved snail, but come and join the dance.
 Will you, won't you, will you, won't you, will you join the dance?
 Will you, won't you, will you, won't you, won't you join the dance?"

# Frog Went A-Courtin'

AUTHOR UNKNOWN

Mr. Froggie went a-courtin' an' he did ride;
Sword and pistol by his side.

He went to Missus Mousie's hall,
Gave a loud knock and gave a loud call.

"Pray, Missus Mousie, air you within?"
"Yes, kind sir, I set an' spin."

He tuk Miss Mousie on his knee,
An' sez, "Miss Mousie, will ya marry me?"

Miss Mousie blushed an' hung her head.
"You'll have t'ask Uncle Rat," she said.

"Not without Uncle Rat's consent
Would I marry the Pres-i-dent."

Uncle Rat jumped up an' shuck his fat side,
To think his niece would be Bill Frog's bride.

Nex' day Uncle Rat went to town,
To git his niece a weddin' gown.

Whar shall the weddin' supper be?
'Way down yander in a holler tree.

First come in was a Bumble-bee,
Who danced a jig with Captain Flea.

Next come in was a Butterfly,
Sellin' butter very high.

An' when they all set down to sup,
A big gray goose come an' gobbled
    'em all up.

An' this is the end of one, two, three,
The Rat an' the Mouse an' the little
    Froggie.

# Simpleton Peter

### RETOLD BY JAMES REEVES

THERE WAS once a young man called Peter, who lived in a country village with his old widowed mother. He was a good-hearted fellow, tall and strong, but he was one of the simplest of men ever born. He could scarcely count his mother's hens, though she had only a score; if he spent threepence out of a shilling, he hardly knew how to work out the change; and as for going to market, he never went without being cheated. It was not for want of trying; it was not because he was lazy; it was just that poor Peter seemed to have been born with scarcely any brains in his head.

"Oh, mother," he would say, "if only I'd been given just a wee bit of brains, I'd not be so much trouble and worry to you."

"Ay, Peter," his mother would say, with a sigh, "you're short of brains, there's no doubt, but you're a good boy, and as strong as any other two, so don't you let it worry you. Now run upstairs and get me three buttons to sew on your jacket, and mind you three is three and not two, nor four neither."

All the same, Peter used to fret about his foolishness. So he continued to pester his mother till at last she said:

231

"Well, if you want to come by some brains, just take a walk to the wise woman who lives on the hill. She's a right clever body, they say, with her magic books and her pills and potions, and perhaps she can help you."

So when his work was done, Peter walked up the hill, and on the top he found the cottage of the wise woman, with smoke coming out of the chimney and a black cat stretched out asleep in the doorway.

"Well, that's a good sign," said Peter to himself, and knocked at the door.

There was no answer, so he lifted the latch cautiously and looked in. There was the old woman, stirring a round black pot on the fire. She neither turned nor said a word, so Peter stepped inside and said:

"Good day to you, wise woman. 'Tis a very fine day, to be sure."

The old woman said nothing, but went on stirring.

"Maybe we shall have rain tomorrow," Peter went on.

But still the old woman said nothing.

"And maybe we shan't," he added, wondering what to say next.

Still the old woman went on stirring.

"Well now," said Peter, "that's all I have to say about the weather, so let's come to business. I'm a very simple fellow, and I came to see whether you could supply me with a wee bit of brains. You see—"

"Brains?" said the old woman, putting down her spoon and turning round for the first time. "Yes, I dare say. That depends on what sort of brains you want. If it's king's brains, or soldier's brains, or schoolmaster's brains, then I can't help you. What sort of brains do you want?"

"Just ordinary brains," said Peter. "Middling good, and middling bad, like most of the folks round here."

"Very good," said the wise woman.

"Such brains you shall have, but you must fetch me the heart of the thing you like above all others. Do you understand? And when you have brought me that, you must answer me a riddle, so that I may tell whether you have really brought the thing I ask for. Now be off with you."

Without waiting for an answer, she took up the pot and carried it into the back kitchen, leaving Peter to let himself out. He went off down the hill, thinking about what the wise woman had said. "The heart of the thing I like above all others," he repeated to himself. "Now what can that be, I wonder?" For this was not the sort of thing Peter usually thought about. When he got home, he told his mother what the old woman had said, and his mother thought the question over. At last she said:

"Why, there's nothing in this world you like better than fat bacon, if you ask me. So we'd best kill the old sow, and you can take its heart to the wise woman."

So the old sow was killed and her heart removed, and Peter took it next evening to the cottage on the hill.

The wise woman was sitting in a chair by the fireplace reading a great book. She scarcely looked up, and Peter put the heart down on the table.

"There 'tis," he said. "The heart of the thing I like best in all the world. Will it do?"

The old woman looked up from her book.

"What is it," she said, "that can run without feet? Tell me that."

"What is it than can run without feet?" repeated the young man, and he

233

scratched his head, and thought and thought till his head ached.

The old woman went on reading. At last Peter spoke.

"I tell you what," he said. "I dunno."

"Well, that's not the thing I asked for," said the old woman. "Take it away and be off with you."

There was nothing for poor Peter to do but pick up the sow's heart and go home again.

When he got near his own cottage, he saw there were people standing about the doorway, and some of the women were crying. Then he learnt that his old widowed mother had been taken suddenly ill and was near death. He went inside the cottage and closed the door. The old woman was indeed very feeble. Peter saw there was nothing to be done, so he knelt by the bedside and took her hand.

"Say good-bye to me, son," she whispered, "for I'm going to leave you. But now you've been to the wise woman and got yourself some brains, you'll be able to look after yourself."

Peter had not the heart to tell her that he had got no brains and had not even been able to answer the wise woman's riddle. Instead, he kissed his mother and said:

"All the same, mother, I shall miss you badly. Good-bye, mother dear, good-bye."

"Good-bye, my son," said the old woman; and with that she closed her eyes, smiled at him faintly, and died.

Peter stayed for a long while kneeling by the bed, crying and crying, for he could not stop the tears from coming. And he thought of all she had done for him—how she had brought him up as a little boy, and healed his cuts when he fell over, and cooked his meals, and mended his clothes, and talked to him, and been company for him in the evenings. He wondered how in the world he would get on without her. "For," he said to himself, "of all creatures in the world, she was the one I liked best."

Then he thought of the wise woman's words.

"Bring me," she had said, "the heart of the one you like best in all the world."

"That I shan't," he said, "not for all the brains on earth."

But next morning he thought he might take his dead mother up to the old woman without taking her heart out, for he was even more in need of a bit of brains than ever. So he put his mother in a sack and took her up the hill. This he did without difficulty, for his mother had been a frail little woman, and he himself was as strong as any two ordinary men. He laid the body down in the wise woman's cottage and said:

"Now this time I have surely brought you the thing I love above all others. Here is my very own dead mother, and now you must give me the brains you promised."

"Tell me this," said the wise woman. "What is it that is yellow and shines and isn't gold?"

"What's it that is yellow and shines and isn't gold?" Peter said.

But he couldn't think of the answer for the life of him, so at last he said:

"I dunno."

"Then you shall get no brains today. You're a simple fellow indeed, and maybe you'll never have any at all."

So Peter took up the sack with his mother inside and went out. But he was too sad to go home; instead, he sat down by the roadside and began to cry.

Presently he heard the sound of a gentle voice at his side. He looked up and saw a handsome young girl watching him with a kindly smile.

"What's the matter?" she asked. "I'm sorry to see a great fellow like you in distress."

"I'm a simple fellow," said Peter, "without any brains, and now my mother has died and left me all alone. So how I'll manage from now on I don't know. There's no one to cook for me and sew for me and manage the marketing, and worst of all, there's no one to talk to me and cheer me up when I'm in trouble."

"I'll help you," said Jenny, for this was the girl's name. "A simple fellow like you shouldn't be without someone to look after him. Will you let me come and look after you?"

"If you like," said Peter, "but you'll find I'm a more than commonly stupid man, unless I can get some brains from somewhere."

"Well," said Jenny, "they say that a foolish man makes the best husband. Will you marry me?"

"Can you cook?" said Peter.

"Yes, indeed," said Jenny.

"Can you sew and mend clothes?"

"To be sure."

"Can you count eggs and add up pounds, shillings, and pence?"

"Well enough."

"Then, if you'll marry me, I'll have you," agreed Peter.

Off they went, and after Peter's mother had been buried and all the village had mourned for her, the two of them were married and made their home together in the cottage. Soon Peter, simple as he was, began to see that he had got a very good wife. She cooked and sewed, mended and washed, all with the greatest cheerfulness and good will. What is more, she kept Peter amused with her witty talk and her gentle ways. Peter was not a bad husband either, for he, too, worked cheerfully and well; nothing was too much trouble for him, so long as he did not have to think; no weight was too much for him to lift, and no distance was too great for him to walk. In short, they were as happy and contented a couple as had ever set up house together in the village.

"Why, Jenny," said Peter one evening, "I believe that of all creatures in the world, you're the one I like the best."

And these words put an idea into his head.

"Surely," he went on, "the wise woman didn't mean me to kill you and take her your heart. Do you think she could have meant that, Jenny?"

"I hope not," said his wife, "indeed I do. Who said anything about killing? Why not take me up to her, alive as I am, heart and all?"

"That's a very good notion," said Peter. "Why couldn't I have thought of it myself? Just you come along with me. But first, you'd better see if you can answer riddles. Tell me, what is it that can run without legs?"

"Why, a river, to be sure," said Jenny. "That's not very hard."

"A river?" repeated the simpleton. "Of course. Now why couldn't I have thought of that? But tell me this: what is it that shines and is yellow, but isn't gold?"

"The sun," said Jenny, without stopping to think. "I could have told you that when I was five years old."

"The sun?" said Peter in a puzzled way. "Yes—that shines, to be sure; and 'tis yellow; and 'tisn't gold neither. Why, what a head you have, Jenny! There can't be a man in all England with a cleverer wife than I have. Come along quickly now, and see if the old woman will give me a little bit of brains, so that I can be more your equal."

So they went up the hill together, and found the wise woman at home.

"Wise woman," said Peter, "at last I've brought you the creature I like above all others. Here she is, heart and all. If you don't give me the brains I ask for now, you're no wise woman, but a cheat and a fraud."

"Sit down, both of you," said the old woman. They sat down, and she turned to Peter and said, "Now then, here's my riddle. What is it that has first no legs, then two, then four?"

Poor Peter thought and thought, but the answer would not come; then Jenny whispered in his ear:

"A tadpole. Say 'a tadpole.'"

"A tadpole," said Peter promptly; and the old woman said:

"Right. Now I see you've got all the brains you want, and they are inside your wife's head. If a man has a clever wife, she is all the brains he needs. Now be off with you, and don't come bothering me any more."

Peter and Jenny got up, thanked the old woman, and went on their way.

As they went down the hill, Jenny was singing quietly to herself, but Peter said nothing.

"What are you thinking of?" she asked gently, stopping in the middle of a song.

Peter left off scratching his head and said nothing. At last he turned to her and answered:

"I was only thinking how proud I am to have such a more than commonly clever young wife. To be sure you told the old woman just what she wanted to know. All the same," he went on in his puzzled way—"all the same, I *can't* see just why it should be a tadpole that has first no legs, then two legs, then four. I've puzzled it out and I've puzzled it out, and still I can't understand. I just can't understand."

# Animal Fables

### RETOLD BY LOUIS UNTERMEYER

## The Foolish Fishes

ONE summer day a man caught some fish. He built a fire of twigs and small branches and brought out a pan. He put some butter in the pan and then placed the fish in the pan. At first the fish did not mind it too much; they liked the feeling along their sides. But when the man put the pan over the fire and the pan began to get hot, they squirmed.

"This is no place for us," cried one of the fish. "Let's get out of here! Let's jump!"

So they jumped—out of the frying pan into the fire. And you can imagine what happened to them!

There's a lesson here for everyone. Don't go from bad to worse. Think twice before you act.

## The Turtle
## Who Talked Too Much

EVER so long ago all the animals talked. And of all the animals, the turtle was the greatest talker. He talked all the time, and to anyone who would listen. Most of his talking was with two geese who lived in the same pond with him.

One day he heard the two geese whispering to each other. "Talk louder," he said. "I can't hear what you are talking about."

"We did not want to frighten you," said one of the geese. "But the pond is drying up. Every day the water gets a little lower, and soon there will not be enough water for us to swim in or even enough to drink."

"I hadn't noticed it," said the turtle. "What are you going to do about it?"

"We are going away," said the first goose. "We are going to fly to a great lake where there is always plenty of water."

"Take me with you," said the turtle. "I don't want to be left behind. I can't live without water. Besides, if I am all alone, I won't have anyone to talk to."

"You talk too much," said the second goose. "And even if we wanted to, how could we take you with us? You can't fly."

"What if I can't fly! You geese are so smart that you should be able to think of some way to take me."

The geese were kind-hearted, and they felt sorry for their talkative friend. They thought and thought of some way to help. Finally they agreed on a plan to take the turtle with them.

"We will take a long, strong stick," they told him. "One of us will hold one end of the stick in our beak, the other will take hold of the other end."

"But what about me?" asked the turtle.

"You will hold on to the middle of the stick with your teeth, and we will carry you through the air until we reach the lake. But remember one thing. Be sure not to say a word. We know how you love to talk. But if you open your mouth . . . well, we don't want to think what will happen!"

"I won't talk. I won't speak," said the

238

turtle. "I won't say a single word. I won't. I promise. I won't."

They found a long, strong stick. The geese took the ends in their beaks and the turtle gripped the middle of the stick with his teeth. Off and away they went, higher and higher, toward the lake.

As they flew over the trees, the turtle wanted to shout, "Here I am—flying!" But he remembered what the geese had told him, and he did not make a sound. When they were over a farm, he felt like calling, "You, down there—look at me, high above all of you!" But, with a great effort, he kept himself from saying it.

Just before they came to the lake, they had to pass over a town, and people in the streets looked up.

"Can we be seeing what we think we are seeing?" the people said to each other. "Is it really a turtle up there? And if it is, what is a turtle doing in the air? It's too funny to be true!"

Hearing this, the turtle lost his temper. He forgot what the geese had told him, and shouted, "There's nothing funny about it! You are just silly people! I tell you a turtle can fly if he wants to! A turtle can do anything he—"

But he never finished the sentence. The moment he had opened his mouth, he had let go of the stick and had started to fall. He fell . . . and he fell . . . and he fell until he hit the ground. No one ever saw or heard from him again because there was nothing left of him.

He had learned his lesson too late. There are times when you should keep your mouth closed.

# The Travelers and the Bear

ONE evening two travelers were walking through the woods. It was dark, and the first traveler said, "I don't like the looks of this place. But there are two of us. We are friends, and if we stick together nothing can harm us."

At that moment a Bear suddenly appeared.

The first traveler yelled and, without a thought for his friend, sprang up a tree. The second traveler, left alone and knowing he had no chance single-handed against the Bear, threw himself down on the ground. He lay flat, not moving a muscle and scarcely breathing. Someone had told him that a Bear will not touch dead meat.

The Bear ambled up to the second traveler, sniffed at him, and nuzzled his head. Then he snuffed at his nose, mouth, and ears. The man never moved. His body was stiff; he held his breath. After a few minutes, the Bear, thinking the man was dead, gave a low growl and shuffled off.

When the Bear had gone, the first traveler came down from the tree.

"Well," he said, laughing, "I noticed that the Bear put his mouth close to your ear. What did he tell you?"

"He told me the truth," said the second traveler. "He told me never to trust anyone who says he will stand by you, and then runs away as soon as there is trouble. You said you were my friend, but a friend in need is a friend in deed."

# The Donkey and the Dog

THERE was once a man who lived quietly in the country. He was not rich, but he had enough money to have a donkey in the stable and a pet puppy in his house. The donkey was very jealous of the little dog.

"It isn't right," the donkey complained. "I do all the work, and that useless dog has all the fun. He is petted and pampered. He gets tidbits from the table. He gets loving pats all day long. He prances about, licks his master's hand, and curls up in his lap. It isn't right!"

One day the donkey made up his mind he would do something about it.

"If the master likes pets so much, I'll be a pet," he said to himself. "That's what I'll be!"

That same day the donkey broke the rope that tied him to his stall and ran out of the stable into the house. He rushed into the room where his master was sitting, pranced around, and kicked up his heels, expecting the master to be delighted. But he was not built to be a pet. His kicking and prancing upset the table, broke the dishes, and smashed all the glasses on the floor. Worse, when he tried to get into his master's lap and lick his face, he threw the chair over; his hooves dug into the master's body and bruised his ribs.

The noise brought in the servants, who gave the poor donkey a terrible beating and whipped him back to the stable.

"Alas," moaned the donkey, "I should be glad to be what I am—a donkey, not a dog. I should have been happy to stay in the stable with plenty of good, healthy hay. Rich tidbits from the table would probably have made me sick."

## Fine Feathers
## Do Not Make Fine Birds

A JACKDAW, a plain black bird a little smaller than a crow, thought himself too good for his companions.

"They say that clothes make the man," he told himself "I must stop going around in this dull black outfit."

Finding some bright feathers that a peacock had shed, he stuck them all over himself.

"Now," said the Jackdaw, "I am well dressed. All the birds will have to admire me." And he strutted like a peacock across the lawn.

But the birds were not deceived. They mocked him and, when he continued to parade in his borrowed plumes, pecked at him until all the fine feathers were torn off.

"I must have made a mistake," he said ruefully. "I ought to go back and stay with my own kind."

But his own kind would have none of him. The other Jackdaws refused to let him join the flock. "You have given yourself too many airs," they said. "We were not good enough for you yesterday. Now you are not good enough for us."

# The Fox and the Stork

THERE was a time when the Fox and the Stork were quite good friends. It was a queer kind of friendship, for the Fox was always playing tricks on the Stork. One day he invited the Stork to dine with him. At dinnertime he placed before his guest nothing but soup in a shallow dish. "Delicious, isn't it?" said the Fox, lapping up the soup and smacking his lips.

The Stork said nothing. Her long bill could not bring up any of the soup, so she sat there while the Fox drank. And the Fox said, "Soup is my favorite food. Too bad you don't like it."

The Stork did not reply for a while. But she was thinking. At last she spoke.

"I don't seem to be hungry tonight," she said when the Fox had finished. "But I would like you to return the visit. Tomorrow night I hope you will come and dine with me."

The next night, when the Fox came to the Stork's house, he sniffed eagerly. Whatever the Stork was going to offer him smelled wonderful. But when the Stork brought it to the table, it was served in a long, thin jar with a very narrow mouth.

"Delicious, isn't it?" said the Stork, dipping her bill into the jar and bringing up one juicy morsel after another.

The Fox said nothing. He could not get his jaw into the narrow opening. He could barely lick the outside of the jar. The joke, he realized, was on him.

*"Seven at One Blow" is one of the fairy tales which,
underneath its fantasy, carries a moral.
From the deeds of the little tailor
the lesson can be drawn that if one has self-confidence
and courage—and a little cleverness—
practically anything may be accomplished.*

# Seven at One Blow

## BY JAKOB AND WILHELM GRIMM

ONCE UPON a time there was a little tailor, small in size, who was always gay in spirit. One day as he sat by the upstairs window, sewing away, a countrywoman came by with a tray of homemade preserves.

"Fine jam for bread," she cried. "Fine jam for bread."

The little tailor was getting hungry; besides, he had a sweet tooth. "Up here," he called. "Come up and show me what you've got."

The countrywoman climbed the stairs with her basket to the tailor's room, and he made her spread out all the pots in a row. He examined them, lifted them up and smelled them. Then he said: "This jam seems good, weigh me four ounces of it, my good woman; and even if it's a quarter of a pound I won't mind." The woman gave him what he wanted, but went away grumbling.

"Now heaven shall bless this jam for my use," cried the little tailor, "and it shall sustain and strengthen me." He fetched some bread out of a cupboard, cut a piece from the loaf, and spread the jam on it. "That won't taste bad," he said; "but I'll finish that waistcoat first before I take a bite." He placed the bread beside him, went on sewing, and out of the lightness of his heart kept on making his stitches bigger and bigger.

In the meantime the smell of the jam rose to the ceiling, where many flies were sitting, and attracted them so that they swarmed on it.

"Who invited you?" said the tailor, and chased the unwelcome guests away. But the flies, who could not understand English, refused to let themselves be driven off, and returned again in even greater numbers. At last the little tailor, losing patience, reached out for a duster, and exclaiming, "Wait, and I'll give it to you," he hit them mercilessly. When he left off he counted the slain; and no fewer than seven lay dead before him.

"What a mighty fellow I am!" said he, and was filled with admiration at his own courage. "The whole town must know about this"; and in great haste the little tailor cut out a belt, hemmed it, and embroidered on it in big letters, "Seven at One Blow." "What did I say, the town? No, the whole world shall hear of it," he said; and his heart beat for joy as a lamb wags his tail.

The tailor strapped the belt round his waist and set out into the wide world, for he considered his workroom too small a field for his bravery. Before he set forth he looked round about him, to see if there was anything in the house he could take with him on his journey; but he found nothing except some old cheese. In front of the house he observed a bird that had been caught in some bushes, and this he put into his wallet along with the cheese. Then he went on his way merrily, and being light and agile he never felt tired.

His way led up a hill, on the top of which sat a giant who was looking over the landscape. The little tailor went up to him, and greeting him cheerfully said: "Good day, friend. You sit at your ease viewing the whole wide world. I'm just on my way there. What do you say to accompanying me?"

The giant looked at the tailor, and said: "What a poor little creature you are!" "That's a good joke," answered the little tailor, and unbuttoning his coat he showed the giant the belt. "There now, you can read what sort of a fellow I am!" The giant read: "Seven at One Blow"; and thinking they were human beings the tailor had slain, he conceived a great respect for the little man.

First he thought he'd test him; so taking up a stone in his hand, he squeezed it till some drops of water ran out. "Now you do the same," said the giant, "if you really wish to be thought strong." "Is that all?" said the little tailor; "that's child's play to me." He put his hand into his wallet, brought out the cheese, and pressed it till the whey ran out. "My squeeze was better than yours," said he.

The giant did not know what to say, for he could not have believed it of the little fellow. To test him again, the giant lifted a stone and threw it so high that the eye could hardly follow it. "Now, my little pygmy, let me see you do that." "Well thrown," said the tailor; "but, after all, your stone fell to the ground. I'll throw one that won't come down at all." He dived into his wallet again and,

grasping the bird in his hand, he threw it up into the air. The bird, glad to be free, soared up into the sky, and flew away.

"Well, what do you think of that little piece of business, friend?" asked the tailor. "You can certainly throw," said the giant. "Now let's see if you can carry a proper weight." With these words he led the tailor to a huge oak tree which had been felled to the ground, and said: "If you are strong enough, help me to carry the tree out of the wood." "Most certainly," said the little tailor. "You take the trunk on your shoulder; I'll bear the top and branches, by far the heaviest part." The giant laid the trunk on his shoulder, but the tailor sat among the branches; and the giant, who couldn't see what was going on behind him, had to carry the whole tree, and the little tailor into the bargain.

There he sat in the best of spirits, whistling a tune, as if carrying a tree were mere sport. The giant, after dragging the heavy weight for some time, could get on no farther, and shouted out: "Hi! I must let the tree fall." The tailor sprang nimbly down, seized the tree with both hands as if he had carried it the whole way, and said to the giant: "Fancy a big lout like you not being able to carry a tree!"

They continued to go on their way together, and as they passed by a cherry tree the giant grasped the top of it, where the ripest fruit hung, gave the branches into the tailor's hand, and bade him eat. But the little tailor was far too weak to hold the tree down, and when the giant let go, the tree swung back into the air, bearing the little tailor with it.

When he had fallen to the ground again without hurting himself, the giant said: "What! Do you mean to tell me you haven't the strength to hold down a feeble twig?" "It wasn't strength that was wanting," replied the tailor; "do you think that would have been anything for a man who has killed seven at one blow? I jumped over the tree because the huntsmen are shooting among the branches near us. Try and do it if you dare." The giant made an attempt, but couldn't get over the tree, and stuck fast in the branches, so that here too the little tailor had the better of him.

"Well, you're a fine fellow, after all," said the giant; "come and spend the night with us in our cave." The little tailor consented to do this and, following his friend, they went on till they reached a cave where several other giants were sitting round a fire, each holding a roast sheep in his hand. The little tailor looked about him, and thought: "Yes, there's certainly more room to turn round in here than in my workshop." The giant showed him a bed, and wished him a good sleep. But the bed was too big for the little tailor, so he crept away into a corner. At midnight, when the giant thought the little tailor was fast asleep, he rose up, and taking his big iron walking stick, he broke the bed in two with a blow, thinking he had made an end of the little grasshopper. At dawn the giants went off to the wood, and quite forgot about the little tailor. Suddenly they met him trudging along in the most cheerful manner. The giants were terrified and, fearful lest he should slay them, they all took to their heels as fast as they could.

The little tailor continued his journey and, after he had wandered about for a long time, came to the courtyard of a royal palace. Feeling tired he lay down on the grass and fell asleep. While he lay there the people came, and looking him all over read on his belt: "Seven at One Blow." "Oh!" they said, "what can this great hero of a hundred fights want in our peaceful land? He must indeed be a mighty man of valor!" They went and told the King about him, and said what a weighty and useful man he would be in time of war, and that it would be well to secure him at any price. This counsel pleased the King, and he sent one of his courtiers down to the little tailor to offer him, when he awoke, a commission in their army. The messenger remained standing by the sleeper, and waited till he stretched his limbs and opened his eyes, when he tendered his proposal. "That's the very thing I came here for," he answered. "I am quite ready to enter the King's service." He was received with all honor, and given a handsomely furnished house of his own.

But the other officers resented the success of the little tailor. "What's to come of it all?" they asked each other. "If we quarrel with him, he'll strike at us, and at every blow seven will fall. There'll soon be an end of us." So they resolved to go in a body to the King. "We are not made," they said, "to hold out against a man who kills seven at one blow." The King was grieved at the thought of losing all his faithful servants for the sake of one man; and he wished heartily that he had never set eyes on him, or that he could get rid of him. But he didn't dare to send him away, for he feared the tailor might kill him along with his people, and place himself on the throne.

He pondered long and deeply over the matter, and finally came to a conclusion. He sent to the tailor and told him that, seeing what a great and warlike hero he was, he was about to make him an offer. In a certain wood of his kingdom there dwelled two giants who did much harm by the way they robbed, murdered, burned, and plundered everything about them. No one could approach them without endangering his life. If, however, he could overcome and kill these two giants he should have the King's only daughter for a wife, and half his kingdom into the bargain; he might have a hundred horsemen, too, to back him up. "That's the very thing for a man like me," thought the little tailor; "one doesn't get the offer of a beautiful princess and half a kingdom every day." "Done with you," he answered. "I'll soon put an end to the giants. But I haven't the smallest need of your hundred horsemen. A fellow who can slay seven at one blow need not be afraid of two."

The little tailor set out, and the hundred horsemen followed him. When he came to the outskirts of the wood he said

to his followers: "You wait here, I'll manage the giants by myself"; and he went on into the wood, casting his sharp eyes right and left about him. After a while he spied the two giants lying asleep under a tree, snoring till the very boughs bent with the breeze.

The little tailor lost no time in filling his wallet with stones, and then climbed up the tree under which they lay. When he got to the middle of it, he slipped along a branch till he sat just above the sleepers. Then he threw down one stone after the other on the nearest giant. The giant felt nothing for a long time, but at last he woke up, and pinching his companion said: "What did you strike me for?" "I didn't strike you," said the other, "you must be dreaming." They both lay down to sleep again, and the tailor threw down a stone on the second giant, who sprang up and cried: "What's that for? Why did you throw something at me?" "I didn't throw anything," growled the first one.

They argued for a time till they were tired; then both fell asleep again. The little tailor began his game once more, and flung the largest stone he could find in his wallet, with all his force, and hit the first giant on the chest. "This is too much!" he yelled and, springing up, he knocked his companion against the tree. He got, however, as good as he gave, and they became so enraged that they tore up trees and beat each other with them, till they both fell dead at once on the ground.

Then the little tailor jumped down. "It's a mercy," he said, "that they didn't root up the tree on which I was perched, or I should have had to jump like a squirrel on to another, which would have been no easy job." He drew his sword and gave each of the giants a thrust or two on the breast, and then went to the horsemen and said: "The deed is done, I've put an end to the two of them. I assure you it has been no easy matter, for they even tore up trees in their struggle to defend themselves; but all that's of no use against one who slays seven at one blow."

"Weren't you wounded?" asked the horsemen.

"No fear," answered the tailor. "They haven't touched a hair of my head." But the horsemen wouldn't believe him till they rode into the wood and found the giants lying in their blood, and the trees lying around, torn up by the roots.

The little tailor now demanded the promised reward from the King. But the monarch regretted his promise, and pondered once more how he could rid himhelf of the hero. "Before you obtain the hand of my daughter and half my kingdom," he said to him, "you must do another deed of valor. A unicorn is running about loose in the wood, and doing much mischief. You must first catch it." "I'm even less afraid of one unicorn than of two giants. Seven at one blow, that's my motto."

He took a piece of cord and an axe with him, went out to the wood, and again told the men who had been sent with him to remain outside. He did not have to search long, for the unicorn soon passed by, and, on perceiving the tailor, dashed straight at him as though it were going to spike him on the spot. "Gently, gently," said he, "not so fast, my friend"; and standing still he waited till the beast was quite near. Then he sprang lightly behind a tree; the unicorn ran with all its force against the tree, and rammed its horn so firmly into the trunk that it had no strength left to pull it out again.

"Now I've caught my bird," said the tailor, and he came out from behind the tree, placed the cord round its neck first, then struck the horn out of the tree with his axe; and when everything was in order led the beast before the King.

Still the King did not want to give the promised reward. He made a third demand. This time the tailor was to catch a savage wild boar that did a great deal of harm in the wood; and he might have the huntsmen to help him. "Willingly," said the tailor. "That's mere child's play." But he did not take the huntsmen into the wood with him, and they were by no means displeased to remain behind.

As soon as the boar caught sight of the tailor it ran at him with foaming mouth and gleaming teeth, and tried to knock him down. But our nimble little friend ran into a chapel that stood near, and got out of the window again with a jump. The boar pursued him into the church, but the tailor skipped round to the door, and closed it securely. So the raging beast was caught, for it was far too heavy and clumsy to spring out of the window.

The little tailor summoned the huntsmen together, that they might see the prisoner with their own eyes. Then the hero went to the King, who was finally obliged, whether he liked it or not, to keep his promise, and hand him over his daughter and half his kingdom. So the wedding was celebrated with much splendor, but little joy, and the tailor became a king.

After a time the Queen heard her husband saying one night in his sleep: "My lad, make that waistcoat and patch these trousers, or I'll box your ears." Thus she learned the truth about the young gentleman, and next day she poured forth her woes to her father. She begged him to help her get rid of a husband who was nothing more nor less than a tailor. The King comforted her, and said: "Leave your bedroom door open tonight. My servants shall stand outside, and when your husband is fast asleep they shall enter, bind him fast, and carry him on to a ship, which shall sail away out into the wide ocean."

The Queen was well satisfied with the idea, but the armor-bearer, who had overheard everything, was much attached to his young master. He went straight to him and revealed the whole plot.

"I'll soon put a stop to this," said the tailor.

That night he and his wife went to bed, and when she thought he had fallen asleep, she got up, opened the door, and then lay down again. Then the little tailor, who had only pretended to be asleep, called out in a clear voice: "My lad, make that waistcoat and patch those trousers, or I'll box your ears. I have killed seven at one blow, slain two giants, led a unicorn captive, and caught a wild boar. Why then should I be afraid of a few men standing outside the door?"

The men, when they heard the tailor say these words, were so terrified that they ran as if pursued by a wild army. So the little tailor was saved and lived to be a king the rest of his life.

# Wynken, Blynken, and Nod

## BY EUGENE FIELD

Wynken, Blynken, and Nod one night
　Sailed off in a wooden shoe—
Sailed on a river of crystal light,
　Into a sea of dew.
"Where are you going, and what do
　　you wish?"
　The old man asked the three.
"We have come to fish for the herring-
　　fish
　That live in this beautiful sea;
Nets of silver and gold have we!"
　　Said Wynken, Blynken, and Nod.

252

The old moon laughed and sang a
　　song
　As they rocked in the wooden shoe,
And the wind that sped them all night
　　long
　Ruffled the waves of dew.
The little stars were the herring-fish
　That lived in that beautiful sea—
"Now cast your nets wherever you
　　wish—
　But never afeared are we."
So cried the stars to the fishermen
　　three:
　　Wynken, Blynken, and Nod.

All night long their nets they threw
　For the fish in the twinkling foam—
Then down from the sky came the
　　wooden shoe,
　Bringing the fishermen home;
'Twas all so pretty a sail, it seemed
　As if it could not be;
And some folks thought 'twas a dream
　　they'd dreamed
　Of sailing that beautiful sea—
But I shall name you the fishermen
　　three:
　　Wynken, Blynken, and Nod.

Wynken and Blynken are two little
　　eyes,
　And Nod is a little head,
And the wooden shoe that sailed the
　　skies
　Is a wee one's trundle-bed.
So shut your eyes while mother sings
　Of wonderful sights that be,
And you shall see the beautiful things
　As you rock in the misty sea,
Where the old shoe rocked the fisher-
　　men three:
　　Wynken, Blynken, and Nod.